Piper met his gaze across the table.

Sure, Gavin McQueen had a strong jawline and a steady dark-eyed gaze.

Gavin stood beside the pergola, talking on his phone. When Izzy tugged at her leash, wanting to be closer to this guy she barely knew, Piper sat on a stone bench and scratched her dog's forehead between the brown eyebrows. "You like him?"

Izzy licked her hand and leaned against Piper's knee. Now they were both staring at Gavin, who seemed to be having a difficult conversation. His fist clenched as if desperately clinging to self-control. He was obviously worried, which made sense. As a lawman, he'd want to protect her. And as a US marshal...

Pieces of the puzzle fell neatly into place. Gavin couldn't talk about the shooting. He had the authority to call on 24/7 guards at the hospital. The other cops deferred to him.

Though she didn't know much about the US Marshals Service, Piper was aware that they monitored the witness protection program. What had her friend gotten himself into?

K-9 HUNTER

USA TODAY Bestselling Author
CASSIE MILES

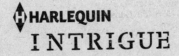

To the dogs—Pookie, Windy, Bear, Dolly, Milo, Cassie and others. And, as always, to Rick.

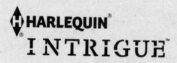

Recycling programs for this product may not exist in your area.

ISBN-13: 978-1-335-59107-4

K-9 Hunter

Copyright © 2023 by Kay Bergstrom

For questions and comments about the quality of this book, please contact us at CustomerService@Harlequin.com.

Harlequin Enterprises ULC
22 Adelaide St. West, 41st Floor
Toronto, Ontario M5H 4E3, Canada
www.Harlequin.com

Printed in U.S.A.

Cassie Miles, a *USA TODAY* bestselling author, lived in Colorado for many years and has now moved to Oregon. Her home is an hour from the rugged Pacific Ocean and an hour from the Cascade Mountains—the best of both worlds—not to mention the incredible restaurants in Portland and award-winning wineries in the Willamette Valley. She's looking forward to exploring the Pacific Northwest and finding mysterious new settings for Harlequin Intrigue romances.

Books by Cassie Miles

Harlequin Intrigue

Mountain Retreat
Colorado Wildfire
Mountain Bodyguard
Mountain Shelter
Mountain Blizzard
Frozen Memories
The Girl Who Wouldn't Stay Dead
The Girl Who Couldn't Forget
The Final Secret
Witness on the Run
Cold Case Colorado
Find Me
Gaslighted in Colorado
Escape from Ice Mountain
Shallow Grave
K-9 Hunter

Visit the Author Profile page at Harlequin.com.

CAST OF CHARACTERS

Piper Comstock—Five years ago, she left her corporate job, divorced her cheating husband and moved to the forests of Oregon where she became a truffle hunter.

Gavin McQueen—As a deputy marshal for the US Marshals Service, he oversees several resettled witnesses and their families in WITSEC (Witness Security Program). Their safety depends on his ability to keep their identities concealed.

Izzy (short for *Isadora*)—A mixed breed (part German shepherd and part poodle), she's trained as a K-9 protector and a tracker. Primarily, Piper's dog is a truffle hound who loves her work.

Chef Marco Barbieri—Relocated in Beaverton, Oregon, after testifying against domestic terrorists in New Jersey.

Sofia Barbieri—Marco's sixteen-year-old daughter who has the voice of an angel.

Yuri Draco—The ninety-four-year-old Dragon is the head of a terrorist gang, currently incarcerated at the federal prison in Sheridan, Oregon.

Chapter One

"Take another sniff." Piper Comstock leaned forward in her chair, rested her elbows on the table and studied the barrel-chested, gray-haired man who sat across from her. Chef Marco Barbieri was as dear to her as her late uncle James, but she wouldn't allow her fondness for the old gentleman to interfere with their negotiation. Marco himself had taught her the basics of bartering. *Always get the best price for your product.*

"Go ahead," she urged. "Inhale."

His bulbous nose twitched. He sniffed again, pursed his lips and patted his ample belly. Satisfied as if he'd devoured a full meal. *"Delicioso."*

She agreed. The fragrance of the Oregon black truffles tickled her nostrils and aroused her senses. Not much to look at, the twelve misshapen lumps—ranging in size from a walnut to a golf ball—were displayed on a glass platter under the hanging pendant lamp in Marco's home kitchen. The truffles she presented to him had been carefully washed and brushed clean. *Handled with care.* She hated to part with these 587 grams of mushroom goodness that she'd harvested from the state forest near her cabin outside Yamhill but keeping the truffles would be foolish. What kind of hunter hoarded her product? This was her job, and she loved it. For confirmation, she reached down to pet her truffle-hunter dog, Izzy.

The current rate for Oregon black truffles ranged from $400 to $600 per pound—a bargain compared to the $2,000 and higher per pound for the prized Alba white truffles from Italy. She had a pound and a quarter. *Not a bad payday.* They'd already haggled to a midpoint. Still, she pushed for more. "It's October, early in the season, but these are perfect and fresh."

"Another fifty." He stood and slapped a neat stack of bills onto the tabletop. He anticipated the price before they'd sat down. To be sure, he'd controlled their negotiation from start to finish, and she bowed to the master.

Piper came around the table and hugged him before she scooped up the cash and tucked it into the billfold in her backpack. "A pleasure doing business, *il padrone.*"

Surprisingly graceful for a big man, he whirled through his kitchen to the marble countertop and grasped the bottle of pinot noir that he'd already uncorked to breathe. After he poured a generous dose into two crystal wineglasses, he toasted her. *"Alla salute, cara."*

Tasting the rich, oaky flavor of the red wine, she licked her lips. "From the winery next door?"

"Sí." He toasted again. "And to you, Izzy."

"A Russian toast?"

"Russian slang."

The black-and-brown dog thumped her tail. Somewhere in her DNA, Izzy—short for Isadora—was German shepherd, which accounted for her markings. Mostly, she resembled a standard poodle with floppy ears, curly fur and a sociable personality. She acknowledged Marco's toast with a cheerful woof.

He laughed. "She's a beautiful mutt."

"The best of each breed." Piper sighed and settled back in her chair, happy to be here with Marco in his charming home in Beaverton not far from Portland. "What delicacies will you make with my beautiful truffles?"

"Carpaccio," he said. "Perhaps a foie gras with pasta or gnocchi. Or a quiche."

Her mouth watered. *Dishes to die for.* "What else?"

"Some will go to Rosa at Bella Trattoria. And, of course, there will be black truffle ice cream for my Sofia."

She'd watched his daughter grow from a coltish young girl to a sixteen-year-old beauty. Six years ago, Piper and Marco had met at a wine tasting in the Willamette Valley. Both had been newly arrived in Oregon. Both recently bereaved. His beloved wife of twenty-two years had passed away. And Piper had divorced her unfaithful, scum-sucking husband.

She shook off that regret-tinged memory and concentrated on thoughts of Sofia, who seemed to be in the throes of teenaged angst. Recently, she'd come along on a truffle hunt and talked about a boyfriend her father wouldn't approve. Not that she expected

Piper to be a substitute mother. More like a favorite aunt. "She's a good kid."

"Not a kid anymore. She's a woman." The old man frowned into his wineglass. "I worry about her."

"It's a father's job to worry," she said. "I'm guessing Sofia can handle herself."

"The boys chase after her. She inherited her mama's raven hair, green eyes and wide smile. When I hear my daughter laugh, I believe my Gina has come back from the dead."

Gina? Piper thought his late wife's name was Angelica. He seldom talked about her, and Piper had never seen a photograph, not a wedding picture or a casual snapshot. She suspected the memories were too painful. "You still miss her."

"Every hour of every day." He massaged his heavy jaw. "I pray for you, *cara mia.* You deserve to find the love of your life."

"I'm not in a hurry."

"Could be any time. Maybe even tonight." He cocked his head to one side. "Maybe take down your ponytail and show off your cinnamon-colored hair. Put on lipstick. Blue eye shadow to match your eyes."

Since Chef Marco had never shown much interest in her appearance, his grooming tips made her suspicious. "Why do you care about eye shadow?" she asked. "I'm beginning to think you have an ulterior motive for our meeting tonight."

He gave an expressive shrug. "I have someone I want you to meet. You'll like him. His name is Gavin

McQueen. Handsome, very handsome. He's strong, honest and smart."

"Uh-huh."

"And he's single."

Typically, Piper didn't do blind dates. Too much could go wrong. "Why is this friend visiting so late? It's almost ten."

"He has an important message. From friends back East." The doorbell chimed and Marco rose from the table. He straightened his shoulders and smoothed the stained white chef jacket he'd worn home from the Bella Trattoria where he worked part-time as *chef de cuisine*. "You will like him, *cara mia*."

"Or not," she muttered under her breath.

As Marco strode down the long corridor to the front door, she took another whiff of the remarkable truffle aroma, much of which would fade in a week to ten days. Only the freshest finds provided the full sensory experience. Since the sixteenth century, these underground mushrooms had been referred to as "black diamonds of the forest" because razor-thin shavings of the odd-looking nuggets enhanced other flavors. Truffles were reputed to have aphrodisiac properties, which she could easily believe because the ephemeral scent made her think of musky sex… and flowers…and fruit…and rich, fertile soil.

Underneath the table, Izzy changed positions, going from a sprawl at Piper's feet to an alert posture. The brown-and-black dog cocked her head to one side, signaling that she was paying attention to the distant echo of Marco's rumbling voice.

Piper gazed into her mutt's intelligent eyes. "I don't need a boyfriend."

"Moof," Izzy said.

"You and me, we're single gals. And we're brilliant together. For sure, you're the world's greatest truffle hound."

Instead of licking her hand and giving her a doggy grin, Izzy growled and stared down the corridor.

"What's wrong, girl?"

The growl deepened as the voices at the end of the hall grew louder. Gunfire exploded. Two shots, one right after the other.

If she'd been alone, Piper would have run out the door to her car and called 9-1-1, but her heroic mutt—trained as an attack dog as well as a truffle hunter—dashed to the rescue, charging toward danger. Piper had no choice but to follow.

Belatedly, she called out. "Izzy, stay."

Izzy barked furiously. Another voice—not Chef Marco's—shouted and cursed. She feared for the old man...and for Izzy. More than a companion, the dog was her well-loved, trusted friend. *And my business partner.* Piper's livelihood depended on the mutt.

She rounded the corner to the front foyer where a wide-shouldered man in a plaid wool shirt over a navy T-shirt with a Yankees logo stood in the open doorway. In his hand, a matte-black gun. Dark brown hair stuck out from his knit watch cap. His face flushed red and his black eyebrows pulled down. He seemed too young to be a killer.

On the entryway floor, Marco curled on his side,

facing away from her. Piper knew he was wounded. Blood pooled around him on the travertine tiles.

"Tell your damn dog to back off." The gunman fired wildly. Attached to the barrel was a long cylinder. A sound suppressor?

She didn't know enough about guns to identify the equipment. If that attachment was supposed to be a silencer, it didn't work. The gunfire was still loud enough that the neighbors would hear. And call the police.

Izzy bounced around the attacker, barking madly. Her usually friendly expression turned ferocious. Her black lips curled in a snarl.

The shooter tried to aim at Izzy. When he gave a panicky shout, she saw that he was missing a front tooth. "Devil dog! Call it off."

His voice held a note of desperation. Piper sensed his fear—a tension that made him as dangerous as a cornered beast. "Don't shoot, please don't shoot."

He swung around. The suppressor pointed at her.

Izzy saw the threat and she reacted. With a flying leap, the mutt launched herself like a furry black-and-brown rocket. She wasn't a huge dog, less than seventy pounds, but her weight combined with the force of her attack toppled the man onto his backside. She clamped her jaws on his forearm, snarling but not biting. She'd been trained not to draw blood unless given the command.

The shooter shouted hysterically but kept his hold on the gun. He reached for a knife sheath attached to his belt.

"If you touch that blade," she said, "my devil dog will rip your arm off."

"Get this damn animal away from me."

"Drop your weapon," she said.

"I hate dogs."

But he did as she said. The handgun clattered on the tiled floor, and she picked it up. Piper infused her voice with authority. "Enough, Izzy. Heel."

Reluctantly obedient, the dog jumped back and took a position at Piper's left side. Izzy showed her teeth. The hackles at the back of her neck flared.

Piper's hands trembled as she clutched the weapon. Before she could figure out how to restrain the shooter and help Marco at the same time, the young man bolted to his feet and took off running. He must have sensed her clumsiness with firearms. Izzy started after him.

To protect her dog, Piper commanded, "Stay."

As she closed the front door, she heard the rumble of a motorcycle engine starting. She hadn't heard the shooter arrive. How long had he been there? Had he been watching them in the kitchen? Dozens of questions rattled in her brain. Why had he attacked? What did he want?

She knelt beside Marco to feel for a pulse. In spite of all the blood he'd lost, his heart still pumped. Izzy snuggled against him and whimpered. His blood smeared the white patch of fur on her chest.

Piper pulled out her cell phone and called 9-1-1. In a few desperate sentences, she gave the situation and the address. Help was on the way. She whispered to Marco, "You're going to be all right."

Her knowledge of first aid was minimal. Never dealt with a gunshot wound before. She remembered something about tourniquets and applying pressure to stop the bleeding. Tearing open his chef coat, she pushed up his sleeveless T-shirt. He appeared to have been shot in the upper left chest and lower on his right side. The second wound might have happened when he'd turned to escape the would-be murderer.

Using a tourniquet wouldn't be possible. She pressed hard against the fleshy area beside the wound on his side. Immediately, her hands were drenched. The cuffs of her denim jacket picked up dark stains. She took it off and used the fabric to stanch the bleeding. "Hang on, Marco. The ambulance is coming."

A groan escaped his lips. "Did you see him?"

The face of the young gunman had imprinted on her brain. Long nose, dark eyebrows and a missing front tooth. Some kind of tattoo on his wrist. "I saw him."

"You must forget his face."

"Believe me, I want to." After her divorce, Piper had chosen to live like a hermit in the small mountain cabin left to her by her uncle. She didn't want to come out of her self-imposed exile, didn't want to be a witness. "Why should I forget?"

"These are dangerous people." Marco clutched her hand. "Take care of my Sofia."

How could Piper have forgotten about his daughter? "Oh my God, where is she? Is she here at the house?"

"Out on a date."

For now, Sofia is safe. Piper struggled to stop the bleeding. Two gunshots at point-blank range did a massive amount of damage. She noticed that he wore a black plastic circle with a tiny, flashing red light on a cord around his neck. Some kind of monitor?

He exhaled a heavy sigh. "It feels like I'm dying."

"No, Marco. You'll be okay."

"It's my time. I'm ready." A cough rattled in his chest. "Soon, I'll be with my Gina. I hear her angel voice calling to me."

"Not yet."

While she continued to apply pressure and offer reassurances, he whispered, "Tell McQueen. It was the grandson."

His muscles tensed in a spasm then released. His eyelids closed as the air drained from his large body, and he seemed to deflate. Unconscious but not dead. His pulse skipped a beat.

"No." Determined, she pressed harder against his chest.

He gasped, struggling for every breath he took.

Izzy tilted back her head and gave a long, mournful wail.

"Stop," Piper commanded. "He's going to be all right."

She wasn't ready or willing to give up hope. Maybe if she believed with all her heart and soul, Marco would recover. She didn't want to let him go.

THE RED LIGHT on the security monitor continued to blink. In spite of several attempts to make contact, Deputy US Marshal Gavin McQueen failed to reach Marco Barbieri. Less than ten minutes away from Barbieri's home in Beaverton, Gavin pushed the accelerator in his unmarked Ford Explorer to top speed, flying along the mostly deserted suburban streets in this heavily wooded area at the outskirts of town. He hoped like hell that Marco and his daughter were unharmed, hidden under the cover of the witness protection program he'd designed for them six years ago.

Yesterday, intelligence from the FBI had caught a hint of danger pertaining to Barbieri's testimony in a counter-terrorism case. Though Gavin had warned him, the old man had blown him off. He hadn't believed, hadn't wanted to believe, that the threat was real. He had, however, agreed to wear the security monitor and to trigger it if there was a threat. Tonight, Gavin was on his way to the house again, hoping to convince Barbieri not to take risks. Being in WITSEC—the Witness Security Program also known as the Federal Witness Protection Program or WPP—meant a new identity and a lifetime of caution. Very few cooperating witnesses had been injured. According to records, none had been killed. Gavin would be damned if a family under his supervision was assaulted. Barbieri and Sofia needed to go on vacation, leave town, disappear for a few days and get away from the autumn rains in Oregon.

The Explorer reached Barbieri's street in Beaverton. Gavin turned onto the long driveway, passing the mailbox at the curb and parking at the three-car garage outside a beige two-story with dark gray trim. The streetlight showed thick foliage with leaves painted rusty red and brilliant yellow. A very nice home. Pricey. When Barbieri had gone into WIT-SEC, he'd paid off every penny of his accumulated debt—as was required in the program because bill collectors were better than vengeful criminals at tracking down people who owed them. Still, the well-known chef had had a small fortune left over, mostly from the sale of his home and his successful restaurant in Jersey City across the Hudson River from Manhattan.

Gavin unlocked the gun safe in his center console and removed his Beretta. Since he was expecting trouble, he didn't bother sliding it into the clip-on holster on his belt.

The beat-up but clean Toyota hybrid Highlander SUV parked in front of the garage made Gavin wonder. What kind of hitman drove a baby-blue vehicle with a dancing mushroom logo on the driver's-side door? Would an assassin drive a hybrid?

From a distance, he heard sirens. An ambulance? Police cars? Somebody had called in an emergency, and he hoped it was Barbieri himself. But if the old man was coherent and alert, why hadn't he answered Gavin's repeated efforts to contact him?

At the front entrance, Gavin twisted the door handle. *Unlocked.* He punched the doorbell and shouted, "Federal marshal."

He thrust the door open. Staying out of the line of

fire, he peeked inside and saw Barbieri—bloodied and unmoving—on the tiled floor. A woman with an auburn ponytail knelt beside him. In her bloodied hand, she clutched a Glock 13 with a suppressor. Tears streaked down her cheeks. This distraught lady sure as hell didn't look like a hit woman, but he wasn't taking any chances. Gently, he said, "I'm US Marshal Gavin McQueen. Put down the weapon. Scoot it over toward me."

Though her hands were trembling, she complied. She was disarmed, but he didn't make the mistake of thinking she was helpless. Beside her, a large, curly-haired dog with markings like a German shepherd stood poised, ready to attack. Between gasps, she asked, "Do you know CPR?"

Gavin picked up her gun and tossed it outside. "Secure your dog."

"She won't attack unless I tell her to."

"Don't you have a leash?"

She shook her head and her eyes narrowed. Anger eclipsed her fear. "I need your help. Marco is still alive."

Gavin looked over his shoulder. The whirling lights of the emergency vehicle cut through the night. "The ambulance is here."

"Thank God," she said.

"Your name?"

"Piper Comstock. I'm here to sell truffles." She wiped at her tears, leaving smears of blood on her cheeks. "This is my dog, Izzy."

"Did you see what happened?"

Chapter Two

When the swarm of police and first responders descended on the pleasant, well-tended home of Marco Barbieri, Piper and Izzy stepped out of the way. They watched the EMTs from the ambulance throw aside her blood-soaked denim jacket and go to work on the unconscious man. A uniformed officer ordered her to wait until someone could take her statement. Someone else wrote down her name and relationship to Marco. Another pointed her down the long corridor toward the kitchen.

Marshal McQueen, who had clipped a silver badge with a five-pointed star to his belt under his black leather jacket, followed her down the hallway. He held her arm as if she needed guiding and direction, which should have annoyed her. She didn't want to like this guy. But his arrogant, take-charge attitude somehow made her feel better. Izzy reflected her feelings. The mutt usually objected to a stranger coming close to her but seemed to like Gavin. In the kitchen, Izzy stood by his side and nudged his hand, shamelessly begging for pets. He complied, scratching between her floppy ears and stroking her curly coat.

"Ms. Comstock, are you all right?"

"No, I'm not." Piper had never seen a person get shot. Marco's blood was all over her. "I have questions for you, so many questions. Who was that person? Why did he shoot Marco? Is he—"

"I'll get answers for you. Will you wait here for me?"

"Do I have a choice?"

"Please stay here in the kitchen. I'll be right back." He gave her shoulder a reassuring squeeze before he strode down the hall. If Piper hadn't been scared and on the verge of going into shock, she would have told him that he had no right to touch her without permission or to give her orders. She was her own boss, not required to answer to anyone. Well, maybe the cops. And probably him, a US Marshal.

Frustrated and angry, her shoulders tensed. This wasn't the way her life was supposed to be. When she moved to Oregon six years ago, she'd expected to find calm, quiet and simplicity. Not that she couldn't handle complications and crisis situations.

Before she'd come here, she'd been a top executive in an Atlanta-based public relations firm where she'd supervised twenty-three employees, handled a four-million-dollar budget and managed dozens of clients. Her job had presented her with massive problems that required decisiveness and organization. Though she'd been fired, it wasn't her fault and she was glad to go.

She'd left the anxiety and the pressure behind, but she hadn't lost the skills she'd learned at Wharton School of Business. Piper could do more—a lot more—than stand around. She knew how to set an agenda.

First order of business: clean up. Setting aside and compartmentalizing her fears about Marco and her worries about Sofia, she went to the double stainless-steel sink in the kitchen and washed Marco's blood from her hands and forearms. *So much blood.* Fear and sorrow coiled through her. *Don't go down that path. Not now.* She concentrated on cleaning up and pulling herself together.

Next item on her agenda: Change clothes. Her brown, short-sleeved T-shirt and her baggy jeans were bloodstained. She couldn't stand to wear them for one more moment.

On a hook by the door to the backyard, she spotted a red hoodie that belonged to Sofia. She grabbed it and went into the bathroom where she slipped off her own shirt and put on the sweatshirt, which ought to be warm enough in the light October chill.

Next task: Taking care of Izzy. That meant going to her car. On her way out the kitchen door, she grabbed a pink-and-yellow-flowered scarf belonging to Sofia and flipped it around her throat. She went around the garage to the front of the house where she froze on the sidewalk, overwhelmed by chaos. Rotating red-and-blue lights flashed through the night. An edge of hysteria ran through the voices and the static communication from police radios.

So many people. So much noise. Her mind went blank. She didn't know what to do until Izzy bumped her leg and nudged her in the direction of her Toyota Highlander. In the back seat, she found Izzy's reflective red dog harness, which was far flashier than any given item in Piper's utilitarian wardrobe. After she fastened the harness straps and hooked up the matching red lead, she felt more in control.

"Ready for the next priority," she murmured as she pivoted toward the house.

Marshal McQueen blocked her way. Streetlights shone on his thick, brown hair and the shoulders of his black leather jacket. The man made a formidable obstacle, and she doubted they'd ever get along. More likely, they'd butt heads. What had ever made Marco think this guy would be a good blind date?

"We're having trouble reaching Sofia," he said. "She's not answering her phone. Do you know where I can reach her?"

"Marco said she was on a date, but her curfew on a Friday night is eleven o'clock, so she ought to be here any minute." She tried to dodge around him, but he didn't budge. "Excuse me. I want to get back to Marco."

"Let the paramedics do their jobs. They've stopped the bleeding and are ready for transport. Nearest emergency facility is eighteen minutes away."

"I'm going with them."

He raised an eyebrow and nodded toward Izzy, who gazed adoringly at Gavin with her pink tongue lolling from the corner of her mouth. "I'm pretty sure the EMTs have a 'no ride-along policy' when it comes to dogs."

"Then I'll follow the ambulance. I don't want Marco to wake up all by himself in the hospital." A horrific thought occurred to her. "What if the man with the gun comes after him there?"

"It's taken care of."

"What do you mean?"

"I assigned armed guards 24/7 while Marco is in the hospital. The best way you can help him is to co-operate with me."

Piper was impressed by the marshal's authority to arrange for guards. He was the man in charge. If she hoped to find the person who shot Marco, she needed to cooperate. "I have something to say that might be important."

"Okay."

"Marco said to tell you it was the grandson. Does that make sense?"

"It does." Concern etched his features.

"Tell me what it means. 'The grandson.' Whose grandson?"

"I can't give you a name."

"Can you at least—"

"Sorry."

The front door of the house swung wide and the EMTs came through. Marco was strapped down on a wheeled stretcher and covered with a blanket. An oxygen mask covered his nose and mouth. When she saw him, broken and helpless, a sob rose from deep inside and caught in her throat. With Izzy at her side, she moved toward the open doors of the ambulance so she could be close to him.

His eyes were squeezed tightly shut, as though in pain. Her heart wrenched as she flashed on the memory of her uncle's death from a heart attack two years ago. *Not Marco, too.* Though he probably couldn't hear her amid all this confusion, she whispered, "You're going to be all right." *I love you, old man. Don't you dare die on me.*

As soon as he'd been tucked inside the emergency vehicle, and the driver pulled away with siren screaming, Marshal McQueen appeared beside her and clasped her elbow. "Come with me."

"No." She yanked her arm away from him. "I'm going to the hospital to wait."

"Sorry, Ms. Comstock, you're not going anywhere for a while. Your car's hemmed in. You have to give a statement to the police and make arrangements to work with their sketch artist. Before that, you need to talk to me."

"Why?"

"Local law enforcement gave me permission to go first. Please come with me."

Much as she despised being coerced, she didn't see a way to get around him. "I need to go to the kitchen first."

"Why?"

She gave a light tug on Izzy's lead. "I need to put away the truffles. This is non-negotiable. It's a top priority."

At the front door, they picked their way through

a collection of police, detectives and CSI personnel. A uniformed officer spoke to McQueen. "We still haven't been able to contact Sofia Barbieri."

"Keep trying."

"Sure thing, Marshal."

She paused at the kitchen table where she and Marco had done their haggling. Some of the crowd from the front of the house had made their way here and meandered through the kitchen. "Is this a crime scene?" she asked. "Is it okay for me to take the truffles?"

"Did the shooter come in here?"

"No."

"Do what you have to do."

Marco had already paid for the truffles, but she could keep them safe until he told her what he wanted to do with the delicate mushrooms. She carefully placed all 587 grams into the insulated carrier that she'd brought with her.

Curious, the marshal watched. "I've never been into truffles. Never tried them."

"Your loss."

"Weird smell."

She met his gaze across the table. Sure, Gavin McQueen had a strong jawline and a compelling dark-eyed gaze. Marco considered him to be handsome and thought they were a good match. He was so wrong. What could she possibly have in common with man who didn't respect truffles?

She zipped the blue-striped carrier. "You asked about Sofia. Is she in danger?"

"I can't tell you."

"Not grammatically correct. You *can* tell me, but you *won't*."

He moved closer and spoke in an undertone. "Yes, she's in danger."

Startled by this unexpected honesty from McQueen, Piper realized that he was doing his job, trying to protect Sofia. And it was up to her to help. She dug through her memory, trying to come up with a clue that might lead to Marco's daughter. "Her boyfriend's name is Logan."

"Last name?"

"Don't know," she said. "I could try calling her on my phone. When she recognized the caller I.D., she might pick up."

"Sofia knows my number," he said. "I've been a friend of the family since they moved to Oregon."

Piper didn't question his statement. He had no reason to lie about his relationship, but she had to wonder about the connection between Marco and Sofia and a federal marshal. "A friend of the family, you say."

"That is correct. Don't you believe me, Ms. Comstock?"

"Since we're both family friends, you can call me Piper."

"Fine." He gave a brisk nod. "I'm Gavin."

His phone rang. "It's her."

He held the screen so she could see Sofia's name. Then he turned and went through the kitchen door into the backyard.

She stared at his leather-clad back as he walked away from her. Apparently, Sofia trusted Gavin enough to call him instead of the police, and Sofia wasn't a sweet, gullible teenager. The marshal was more than a casual acquaintance.

Piper tugged on Izzy's lead and exited the kitchen into the terraced, landscaped backyard bordered by red maples and sumacs that had already begun to lose their leaves. A light rain misted the darkness where strategically placed lights shone on a rose garden, rows of unharvested autumn vegetables and a patch of fresh herbs. Gavin stood beside the pergola, talking on his phone.

When Izzy tugged at her leash, wanting to be closer to this guy she barely knew, Piper sat on a stone bench near the roses and scratched her dog's forehead between the brown eyebrows. "You like him?"

Izzy licked her hand and leaned against Piper's knee. Now they were both staring at Gavin, who seemed to be having a difficult conversation. His fist clenched as if desperately clinging to self-control. He was obviously worried about Sofia, which made sense. As a lawman, he'd want to protect her. And as a US marshal…

Pieces of the puzzle began to fall into place. Gavin couldn't talk about the shooting or about Marco and Sofia. He had the authority to call on 24/7 guards at the hospital. The other cops deferred to him. Though she didn't know much about the US Marshals Service, Piper was aware that they managed the witness protection program.

Six years ago, when she'd met the Barbieri family, Piper had been escaping the disaster her life had become. Maybe Marco and Sofia had also been on the run.

THE MAIN PART of Gavin's job included monitoring twenty-seven protected witnesses in the Portland area. Marco Barbieri—real name Maxim Lombardi—and his daughter were among his favorites. Unlike ninety-three percent of those in WITSEC, they weren't career criminals who'd ratted out their former associates. The Barbieris, having been in the wrong place at the wrong time, had made a conscious decision to contact the FBI with information that derailed a terrorist plot involving Newark Liberty International Airport. In Gavin's opinion, Marco's actions defined true heroism, but the chef never had a parade in his honor or received a medal. Instead, he got WITSEC—a program that required him to leave behind his friends, family and livelihood.

Gavin remembered the first time he'd seen ten-year-old Sofia—a gutsy kid wearing a bedazzled jean jacket over hot pink leggings, her long black hair pulled up in two ponytails. He saw the glitter of anger in her emerald-green eyes. Clearly, she'd hated leaving behind her friends, her school and her beautiful home. Gavin also saw that she'd understood the danger, loved her papa and would do anything for him.

The child had been mature beyond her years. Now she was a teenager. Headstrong, demanding, and impossible.

He wanted to wait until they talked face-to-face before he explained the seriousness of Marco's wounds. Over the phone, he only said that Marco was in the hospital. "Tell me where you are, and I'll pick you up."

"Will you take me to see him?"

"I can't make any promises, but I'll try."

"What happened to him?"

"You know how this works, Sofia. I can't give you too much information. Let me pick you up."

"Then what?" She swore under her breath, too quietly for him to make out the words but loud enough for him to know she was furious. "Let me guess. You're going to stash me away in some skeevy motel room with a loser bodyguard."

"I'll stay with you."

"As if that's supposed to make me feel better?" She scoffed. "Have we been... What's it called? Have we been compromised?"

She knew he couldn't talk to her about the inner workings of the WITSEC program and the danger that would surround her for the rest of her life. For her own good, he needed to keep the details to himself. The less she knew, the better. "Give me your location."

"I'm telling you right now, Marshal McMeanie, I'm not going to move again. People are starting to notice my music. And I have a boyfriend, a serious boyfriend."

Mentally, he ran through a series of his own curses, profanity that would make a sailor weep. This conversation would have been easier if he could have told Sofia that her father had been shot point-blank in the chest, and the bad guys were coming for her. Either she could listen to him or risk her life. "You haven't told this serious boyfriend about WITSEC, have you?"

"How dumb do you think I am?" Though her melodic voice remained in control, he could hear the strain. "Tell me exactly what happened to my papa. Or I'm going to hang up."

"Don't hang up." He glanced toward Piper and Izzy. Piper had known about the boyfriend. Maybe she could help. "There's someone here who can talk—"

"'Bye, Gavin."

The connection was broken. His grip on the phone tightened as though he could squeeze information from the plastic and circuits. A few weeks ago, he'd put a tracker on Sofia's phone, but she'd found the device, disabled it, and scolded him about spying on her. The kid was smart about technology, too smart. Sure, the tech wizards could download her phone calls and ping her location, but that sort of tracking took time. He needed to get Sofia into protective custody immediately.

Piper came over to him. "I remembered a few details about Logan."

"Tell me."

"Sofia didn't think her dad would approve of their

relationship. Logan's family lives in a commune outside Beaverton. Some people think it's a cult."

"Is Sofia there with the boyfriend?"

"It's very possible," she said.

"Do you know where it is?"

"Not exactly. The person who runs the commune is Chris Offenbach."

He needed to check this commune out and preferred to take a low-key approach. Visions of the debacle at Ruby Ridge raced through his mind. Dealing with a cult could be dangerous. "Are they armed?"

"According to Sofia, they're not militant," Piper said. "They want to drop out of society and take care of themselves. They raise chickens and goats. And they have a vegetable garden. They're preppers—people who hoard food, water, medicine and whatever to prep for any disaster. Sofia told me they have a communal warehouse that's stocked as full as a grocery store."

"Great. Perfect. Wonderful." He sent a text message to Inspector Marshal Beekman, the computer expert in the Portland office of the US Marshals Service, to get information about the prepper commune near Beaverton. "Are all teenage girls so unreasonable about their boyfriends?"

"Ever since Shakespeare. Juliet was thirteen, you know. And Romeo, sixteen."

When he slipped the phone into his pocket, Izzy brushed his thigh and looked up expectantly. Unable to resist the doggy charm, Gavin stroked her soft, curly fur. He was about to make a decision he might regret, namely bringing Piper with him to find Sofia. The way he figured, Piper was already involved, already a witness.

He cleared his throat. "Sofia's angry at me and might be more likely to talk with you. I want you and Izzy to come with me."

"What happened to the other stuff I'm supposed to do? Like giving a statement. And talking to a sketch artist."

"You mentioned priorities," he said. "This is number one—keep Sofia safe."

Izzy gave a quiet woof of agreement.

Chapter Three

After he'd loaded Piper and Izzy into his unmarked Ford Explorer, Gavin returned to the house and switched into administrative mode. Lots to do. Not enough time to do it all.

In his position as a US marshal, primary jurisdiction for the investigation and the pursuit of the suspect fell under his purview. Checking his tactical watch, he noted that nineteen minutes had passed since he'd arrived on the scene. Too damn long. He needed to find that smartass sixteen-year-old before the shooter figured out where she was.

He told the Beaverton police detective in charge that Deputy Marshal Dan Johnson would arrive momentarily with a team to process the scene, including a forensic expert. Probably a waste of time. He doubted forensics would turn up much in the way of physical evidence because a mob of first responders had tracked in loose soil and the leafy detritus that was unavoidable during the October rainy season. Still, the forensic team from the US Marshals Service had to make an effort to sort through the tire tracks, footprints and fingerprints. And, of course, they needed to take the Glock 13 and sound suppressor for ballistic processing. Also, Marshal Johnson would organize the necessary questioning of the neighbors. Had they noticed anyone hanging around in the neighborhood? Or a strange vehicle parked on the street? When they were out walking their dog, did they overhear an argument?

In the back of his mind, Gavin counted down the passing seconds. They needed to get moving. He informed the local police that he and Piper were taking off, but he'd make sure she stayed in touch to give a more detailed witness statement and sit with a sketch artist.

He did *not* share details about where they were going. The locals didn't need to know about Sofia and the commune where she might be holed up with the guy she said was "special." This Logan kid must be pretty damn special since she'd chosen him instead of being with her papa in the hospital. True, Sofia didn't know how serious Marco's injuries were, but still...

After he maneuvered his Explorer through the tangle of other vehicles parked in front of Marco's house, he pulled over and parked at a curb in the quiet Beaverton suburb. A blanket of silence cushioned the interior of the vehicle while a light rainfall splattered the windshield. He inhaled and filled his lungs with cool, humid air. In the light from the dashboard, he saw Piper in the passenger seat and Izzy in the back. Both watched him with expectant eyes.

"Why are we stopping?" Piper asked.

"I have a location." His phone in his pocket had buzzed. The ever-efficient Inspector Beekman had texted him with details about the survivalist commune near Beaverton.

When he started reading to himself, Piper loudly cleared her throat. "I'd like to hear about this place. I might have something useful to add. I'm not a prepper or anything, but I understand what it means to live off the grid."

Since Beekman tended to ramble through an overload of statistical data, Gavin summarized the basics. "The sixty-acre property belongs to the Offenbach Community Farm Project, which is owned by Chris Offenbach. This commune isn't welcoming but isn't considered an existential threat."

"Got it," she said. "Lots of No Trespassing signs, but they aren't stockpiling rifles or smuggling contraband."

"They have their own generators, water supply and waste disposal." He scrolled through Beekman's detailed listing of amps, permits and supplies. "Twenty-four to twenty-seven families live in separate cabins."

"Bigger than I thought," Piper said.

"Here's the bad news. There aren't addresses or numbers on those cabins. No way of telling which family lives in which house."

"If Sofia is there, she could be in any of those cabins."

"Correct," he said.

"Does the text give directions to the farm?"

"Beekman included a GPS display of the fastest route."

Gavin fastened his cell phone into a holder above the center console and merged onto the quiet suburban street. According to the map on his phone, the Offenbach community farm was about fifteen miles from their current location following a series of twisting roads. Didn't seem like it would be difficult to find the place. Discovering the cabin where Sofia was hiding with her special boyfriend presented the real challenge.

From the middle row of his Explorer, Izzy braced her front paws on the center console, poked her head between the bucket seats and stared through the windshield as though she knew where they were headed and why. Piper reached over and scratched under the dog's chin. "Sorry, pup, we're not going out to hunt for truffles."

"I'd like to see her do her job."

"She's impressive," Piper bragged. "Izzy sniffs around the forest, dashing from tree to tree. When she finds a truffle, she puts her front paws down and sticks her butt up in the air, like the yoga pose for Downward-Facing Dog."

To emphasize Piper's words, Izzy leaned over and gave Gavin a lick on the neck. "That tickles." He chuckled. "She's my kind of mutt."

She panted and licked him again.

Gavin didn't usually work with a partner...or a dog. Contact with witnesses in the program had to be tightly monitored within the law enforcement community, even more so with civilians. Mario and Sofia's relationship with Piper was a good example. Marco had reported a friendship with her about five years ago, which meant Gavin had checked her out to make sure she wasn't involved in criminal activity. Her file had been pristine. He remembered the first time he'd seen her photo on a business ID from the Atlanta PR firm where she'd worked. With her auburn hair sculpted into a tidy bob and her heart-shaped face expertly painted with makeup, she'd looked fashionable and stunning. He preferred her currently disheveled appearance with strands of hair falling down from her ponytail and freckles across her nose.

In any case, having Izzy and Piper with him went against regulations. He rationalized that he'd brought them along because they'd witnessed the shooting and might have information that would lead to the capture of the "grandson" who'd attacked Marco. The true reason he'd recruited them was simpler: he was using her to reassure Sofia. Not a bad thing. The fuzzy mutt amused him, and Piper appealed to him on several different levels. He admired her courage and the depth of her commitment to Marco and his daughter. She'd saved the old man's life with her admittedly clumsy attempts at first aid. At least, she'd rolled up her sleeves and tried.

Glancing past Izzy's nose, he noticed a long, wavy lock of dark ginger hair had slipped loose from Piper's high ponytail and curled past her cheekbone. Definitely an attractive woman, he wondered why she lived alone in the forest. Her background raised more questions than answers. A graduate of the prestigious Wharton School of Business didn't typically end up as a truffle hunter in the Oregon forests. And what was the reason for her supposedly no-fault divorce?

Following the GPS directions through the light rain, he guided the SUV west on a main road bordered by thick forest with heavy moss clinging to the tree trunks. A full moon peeked through the cloud cover.

"What's it like to be a marshal?" she asked.

Hold on. It was his job to ask questions. "I'm just like any other law officer."

"Not really. Marshals are kind of legendary, like Wyatt Earp. The movie version is a little bit glamorous when selflessly tracking down a notorious fugitive."

"How did you learn about marshals?"

"You have your tech wizard, Marshal Beekman. I have Google." She ducked around Izzy to look at him. "Also, you're the ones who handle witness protection. What do you call it? WITSEC? Wait, maybe I got it wrong. Is the FBI involved? Do you work with the feds?"

Her conversation skirted the edge of what he could legitimately talk about. "Who told you I work for WITSEC?"

"Logical deduction," she said. "Right away, I knew you were a marshal. When we met, you shoved open the door, stuck a gun in my face and yelled, 'Federal marshal.' Which, by the way, is not how a blind date usually behaves."

"Blind date?"

"Didn't Marco tell you? He thought we'd be a good match." Her eyebrows lowered as she stared at him. "Is Marco even his real name? Earlier tonight, he spoke of his late wife—whose name is Angelica— as Gina. Why aren't there photos of her? No family photos at all. He never mentioned the name of the restaurant he owned. And Sofia never talks about friends from back East. Where's back East? Manhattan? Boston?"

Wondering if it was too late to drop her off at the side of the road, he took a sharp left onto a nearly invisible two-lane road. Izzy slipped from her perch on the console, bounced around in the rear seat and clambered back into position.

"Here's the deal," Gavin said. "The whole point of witness protection is secrecy. If I shoot off my mouth about my job and the people I work with—"

"Like Marco and Sofia?"

"I never mentioned their names."

"But it's obvious you're protecting them."

How many ways did he have to tell her to back off? Rather than say too much, he switched topics. After a glance at the digital dashboard clock, he said, "It's past eleven thirty. That's after curfew for Sofia. Is she usually prompt?"

"Keeping in mind that she's a teenager prone to acting out, she's reliable. And she loves her papa."

Piper shrugged. "I can't believe she didn't come running when you told her what happened."

"I said Marco was in the hospital. Didn't mention that he'd been shot."

"What?" She jolted as far forward as her seat belt would stretch. "Why not?"

"I wanted to speak to her in person." A less noble reason had prevented him from saying too much. He admitted, "I need to control her response. She might not be allowed to see him."

"That's not right." Piper shook her head so vigorously that another strand of hair tumbled loose. "It's cruel. How can you keep her apart from her father?"

Frustration bubbled inside him, urging him to speak up and tell the truth. Lying and secrecy never came easily to him, but those were the necessary tools to ensure the survival of his witnesses. "If she goes to her father, the shooter will know where to find her. He can lurk around outside the hospital door on his motorcycle, waiting for her to come out, waiting for us to make the wrong move. And Sofia pays the price. She could be the next target for assassination."

"Surely, she's not a witness. She was only ten when they moved here."

"I'm not going to talk about it."

"What about me?" she asked. "I saw the shooter's face. Like it or not, I'm a witness. Will I have to go into WITSEC?"

Gavin had been shuffling this possibility in his mind like a deck of cards. Piper's situation was different because "the grandson" hadn't committed murder and wasn't a domestic terrorist. Still, she might be in danger. "We'll have to discuss this later."

"What are my options? I deserve to know."

"There's nothing more to say. Not at the present time."

Cold silence filled the SUV while he drove along the indicated route toward the Offenbach property. The twisting gravel road was fairly well maintained, which he took as a good sign. A more dangerous commune would have made the approach more treacherous.

"Okay, I'm sorry," she said quietly. "Your job sounds incredibly intense and stressful and…lonely. I understand."

"Do you?" He couldn't resist taking a jab. "Is that what it's like to be a hotshot executive at a PR firm?"

"How did you know about that?"

"I'm an investigator. I investigate." He checked the map on his phone screen. "The commune is around the next curve in the road."

"I know how we can figure out which cabin Sofia is in." She untwined the flowered scarf draped around her neck. "I borrowed this from Sofia."

"When?"

"After I cleaned up and grabbed this red sweatshirt. The scarf goes with it. Lucky break."

He wasn't following her reasoning. "What are you suggesting?"

"Izzy's sense of smell is over 10,000 times better than ours, probably more like 100,000."

"How is that possible?"

"Here's how it was explained to me. If you or I glance into a forest, we'll see more shades of green than we have words to describe. A dog's olfactory sense has a similar capacity to identify variations in aroma," she said. "Also, Izzy is a born hunter. This is a game to her, and she likes to win. If I give her a whiff of the scarf, she'll find Sofia."

"Isn't your smell on it?"

"Well, duh. Give the mutt some credit, will you? She can see I'm standing right here. The main smell on the scarf belongs to Sofia. Izzy can track her."

A much better idea than randomly knocking on doors in the middle of the night. As the SUV rounded the curve, he saw a string of rough-wood fence posts with chicken wire stretched between them, marking a long boundary line into the forest. Though a wooden gate blocked the road at an entrance, the purpose didn't appear to be security. No padlock on the gate. Just an easily opened latch and a No Trespassing sign.

"Not a great deterrent to gate-crashers," Piper said.

"The fence isn't to keep people out." He pointed to two small, spotted black-and-white goats who meandered at the edge of the fence, compelling Izzy's immediate attention. "It's to keep the livestock in."

"Should I unlatch the gate?" she asked.

"We'll leave the SUV here and walk. If we drive through, we'll wake up everybody in the commune."

He pulled to the side of the road and put the

Explorer in park. If Sofia and her boyfriend were here, he wanted to get her away and into a safe, secure location as quickly as possible. Marco would be outraged if he knew his daughter was hanging out with people who might be part of a cult.

Even though Beekman had assured him these survivalists weren't dangerous, Gavin had doubts. Most people who sequestered themselves in the forest weren't fond of marshals or other law enforcement personnel. Again, he thought of Ruby Ridge, an essential part of the US Marshals history and lore. That eleven-day siege in 1992 had started with an attempt to serve a warrant and escalated to a shootout that validated the claims of militia groups who had declared war on the government. A deputy marshal had been killed.

A tragic legacy Gavin refused to repeat.

Chapter Four

Though Gavin had great respect for K-9 Search and Rescue Units, he wasn't sure what to expect from a mixed-breed goofball like Izzy. Piper came around the vehicle, carrying her backpack and holding a long leash attached to Izzy's flashy red harness.

"Heel," Piper said in a deep, authoritative voice.

Izzy glanced over her shoulder at the spotted goats and tugged at the leash, obviously annoyed that she wouldn't be allowed to play.

"Heel."

Tail dragging, Izzy went to Piper's left side and sat. She stared longingly at the bleating kids but stayed in position while Piper took a gallon jug and a collapsible bowl from her pack. She splashed a few cups of water into the bowl for Izzy.

"Following a scent can be dehydrating," Piper said. "I need to make sure she's ready."

"Is she trained as an SAR dog?"

"We've taken a couple of classes." Piper shrugged and picked up the bowl after Izzy had slurped her fill. "She's brilliant, picked up the necessary skills right away. It's mostly about scent."

"Have you always been a dog person?"

"I never had pets when I was growing up. My mom was very tidy, very organized, and didn't want the mess. And my dad, well, he's an absent-minded professor who can barely remember to brush his teeth. Not a good one for taking care of a dog."

"How did you get Izzy?"

"My uncle James gave her to me for protection when I first moved to the cabin. She was a year and a half old and already trained as an attack dog—a skill that came in handy when we confronted the man with the gun."

"You said Izzy took him down."

"Damn right she did." Piper grinned proudly. "She's a good protector but more of a lover than a fighter. Her fierce German shepherd attitude gets mixed up with her tender-hearted poodle side. Do you remember Pepé Le Pew from the cartoons?"

"Sure, the sex-crazed, French skunk."

"Izzy is more that type. Anyway, I could see from the start that my curly-haired mutt had tons of potential, and I had the time to train her. Hours and hours with nothing to do. Free time."

A wistful tone in her voice hinted that she might be lonely. He wondered how long she'd been sitting in her cabin, talking to no one and storing up all these words that came gushing out of her. When he first arrived at Marco's house, he requested an updated background check from Beekman and learned that her uncle, James Comstock, passed away two years ago. She had no other family nearby. Piper didn't go to work in an office, not anymore. According to Beekman's report, she made the bulk of her income selling online software designed for businesses of all sizes, ranging from international to neighborhood. Her best friend and companion, it seemed, was her dog.

She continued. "Izzy loved tracking, which led to classes with SAR, and we occasionally volunteer in searches for missing persons. The SAR instructors pointed me toward truffle hunting. And there you have it, the full résumé."

"Izzy has many skills."

"Not to mention that she's super cute." Piper emptied the last bit of water from the bowl and tucked it into her pack. "Let's go find Sofia."

He unlatched the gate so they could enter the commune. Well-spaced LED lights on aluminum poles provided enough illumination to get around without using his pocket-sized Maglite. Maybe the people who lived here weren't felons, but Gavin still didn't want to attract unnecessary attention. The two-lane road swooped into a circle that surrounded a landscaped central area with a covered, gazebo-style bandstand and benches. At the far end of the circle was a sprawling, two-story cedar house with three gables. On the covered porch that stretched across the front, several Adirondack chairs and side tables were arrayed.

On either side of the circle were four cabins—

prefab cedar of varying designs. Cars and trucks were parked in front or tucked into attached garages.

The community farm spread out from this central area. Beyond the two-story house, he spotted a traditional-style barn with a sloping tin roof. Additionally, he saw a long, low horse stable with an attached corral. They were too far away to get a good look at the fields, but Gavin supposed that most of the crops had already been harvested. No doubt, the apples, cherries and peaches had also been picked. The Offenbach Community Farm Project didn't match his idea of a cultlike militia organization. This place couldn't have been more wholesome. If it hadn't been close to midnight, he wouldn't have hesitated to knock on doors and ask for help in finding Sofia.

He turned to Piper. "How do we start the search?"

She crouched beside her mutt and spoke to her in a calm tone. "Izzy, pay attention. We want to find Sofia. You remember Sofia. She gives you treats. Okay, here's her scarf."

Gavin withheld his natural skepticism as he watched Piper hold the scarf for Izzy to sniff. With more than twenty-four cabins and no guarantee that Sofia had stayed in just one, the odds of locating her by scent were against them.

Piper stood. "Seek, Izzy. You can do it. Find Sofia. Seek."

The mutt put her nose close to the ground and started ranging toward the houses on the right side of the circle. Izzy didn't waste time going all the way

up the sidewalks to the front doors. Quickly, she rejected one house after another. At the upper edge
of the circle, she crossed to the left side and did the
same maneuver.

The baby goats had noticed Izzy's search and
joined her, one on each side, bleating loudly. Gavin
feared they'd attract attention. "Can you direct Izzy
toward a more open area? There are plenty of cabins
behind these."

"It's best to let her choose which way to go."

Izzy headed toward a simple cabin close to the
large central house. The goats pranced beside her,
making a racket. It was no big surprise when the
porch light came on. Gavin had hoped to complete
this search without rousing the people who lived
here. He lowered his hand to the holster clipped to
his belt and slapped a congenial smile on his face.

A man with unlaced, battered work boots stepped
heavily onto the small porch. He hooked his thumbs
in the straps of his saggy overalls, pushed the greasy
black hair off his forehead and scowled. "What the
hell?"

"Sorry to bother you, sir." Gavin tried to stick as
close to the truth as possible. "We're looking for a
young woman who is visiting here. Her father is in
the hospital."

"Uh-huh." He folded his scrawny arms across his
equally scrawny chest and leaned against the door-
frame. "What are you doing with that dog?"

"She's helping us search."

"Are you a cop?" His beady eyes narrowed. "I don't much like cops."

Gavin hoped this guy was an aberration, not typical of the gentle farm folk he'd been told lived here. "Thanks for your time, sir."

"Hey," the man shouted toward the neighboring cabin. "Clemmons and Richter, get out here. There's a damn cop asking questions."

As if they'd been waiting for his summons, two other men swaggered onto the porch of their slightly larger cabin. A short, pudgy guy with a thick red beard carried a sawed-off shotgun at his side. The tall, rangy man who followed him resembled a young Abe Lincoln but wasn't as articulate. He barked one sentence. "Get off our land."

These three could be the start of a mob, and Gavin didn't want to provoke them, didn't want to draw his Beretta. But he wasn't going to run away. He stood his ground as they left their porch stoops and approached him. Their palpable hatred cut through the light mist. What were they hiding? What were they trying to protect?

Young Abe grabbed his arm and Gavin quickly wrenched free. He lowered his voice. "I don't want any trouble."

"Listen to this guy," Abe crowed. "He don't want trouble."

"You'd better do what we say." Redbeard cocked his shotgun. "Grab your girl and your dog and get out of here. I mean now."

Gavin turned to look for Piper. She'd followed

Izzy, who continued to sniff the earth and move with determined speed toward the large house at the top of the circle. Izzy planted her front feet on the porch, stuck her rear end in the air and wagged her tail.

"Over here," Piper called out. "We found her."

Gavin was itching to pull out his badge and arrest these knuckleheads. Probably the worst move he could make. Instead, he sidestepped toward Piper while keeping his eyes on the three angry men who followed, muttering dark insults and laughing among themselves.

The front door to the big house crashed open. A short woman with spiky white hair stepped outside and aimed her long, black Remington rifle at them. "I'm Chris Offenbach and this is my land. What do you think you're doing here in the middle of the night?"

For the second time in one day, Piper found herself staring down the bore of a lethal weapon. Not an event she wanted to become habitual. A shudder went through her, and her blood ran cold, but she wasn't truly afraid. Not like when she'd seen Marco bleeding on the floor. Piper understood exactly what this small woman with the big gun was thinking. Chris Offenbach, owner of the Offenbach Community Farm Project, was annoyed. And who could blame her? Not Piper, that was for sure. She hated when people showed up on her doorstep uninvited.

She squeezed her eyes shut, opened them wide and hoped she was correct. "I'm sorry we disturbed you, Ms. Offenbach. We're looking for someone. A missing girl."

Izzy added a doggy exclamation point, thumping the floorboards of the porch with her tail and looking up at the spiky-haired lady with the long gun.

Immediately, Chris lowered her rifle, beamed at Izzy and said, "Well, now, aren't you a fuzzy-wuzzy honey bun?"

Izzy thumped faster.

"Yes, you are." Chris spoke in singsong baby talk. "You're a cutie patootie."

Hearing the angry grumble of the three men surrounding Gavin, Piper looked over her shoulder at them. It'd take more than a tail wag from Izzy to calm these backwoods thugs. The short one with the red beard shouted, "We've got to get rid of these damn people, Chris."

"Yeah," his taller buddy agreed. "The guy's a cop."

Chris went down on one knee to pet Izzy on the head and stroke her soft, curly coat. "I haven't got a problem with law enforcement, not as long as they're friends of this pretty girl."

"Best friends," Piper said, honestly describing her relationship with her mutt. "Her name is Izzy, short for Isadora."

"Are you a policewoman? You don't look like one."

"I'm a truffle hunter."

Still fussing over Izzy, Chris raised her dark eyebrows toward her silvery hairline and focused her sharp ebony gaze on Piper. "You don't say? I'd like to learn how to do that."

"I can teach you. As long as you have a dog with the right kind of personality. You know, obedient and smart and full of energy."

The thug in the overalls scoffed. "This is a bunch of baloney, Chris. We don't want the law in here."

"Why not?" Gavin asked in a calm but serious tone. "Have you got something to hide?"

Overalls took a long stride forward and purposely bumped Gavin in the back. "You better shut the hell up."

When Gavin whirled to face him, Piper could tell from his clenched fists and tight jaw that the marshal was restraining himself. Through gritted teeth, he repeated, "What are you hiding?"

"This is none of your business," Overalls said. "Not in the least."

For the first time, Piper noticed an accent. Russian? Marco occasionally used Russian phrases. She worried that there might be a connection between these men and her friend. Had she and Gavin flipped from the frying pan into the fire? If so, Sofia could be in even more danger than they'd imagined.

"What's your name?" Gavin demanded.

"I don't have to tell you."

"Scared?"

"Dmitri," Overalls growled. "They call me Dmitri."

On the porch, Chris straightened to her full height, which was maybe an inch over five feet. "Settle down, gents. I've heard your complaints, and I'll give them all the consideration they deserve. In the meantime, go home and get some shut-eye. Izzy and her friends are coming inside with me."

Dmitri snarled. "What makes you think you can tell us what to do?"

"Well, let's see." She pursed her lips and widened her eyes. "I'm your landlady and can evict you from your cozy little cabins. Also, I can cut off access to free food and other products we make."

"You're right, Chris." Redbeard lowered his shotgun and backed down. "We've got no problem. Just trying keep our noses clean, you know. No troubles."

Sensing a lull in the hostilities, Piper darted up the stairs to the porch and went through the open door into the house. She watched Gavin follow at a slow, regulated pace, as if to show the other men he wasn't being pushed around. Izzy and Chris brought up the rear.

The cozy, rustic interior of the two-story house featured sturdy furniture with a tawny leather couch, rockers, hand-carved end tables with totem pole legs and overstuffed chairs upholstered in shades of orange, red and black—a color scheme that was reflected in pillows and in the woven rugs scattered across the polished hardwood floors. A fieldstone fireplace rose two stories in the wide-open front room that was traversed by a carved wooden stair railing and banister across the second floor. Bonsai trees, pottery from Pacific Northwest tribes and handcrafted items gave an overall effect of artistic individualism without being cluttered.

Piper's gaze darted from a carved spirit mask from the Tlingit tribe to a framed prairie star quilt to a landscape painting of Mount St. Helen's before the 1980 eruption. "You have quite a collection."

"Not an artist myself, but I appreciate the skill."

"This is a big house. Do you live here alone?"

"Just me and my son." She exhaled a sigh. "My husband passed away eight years ago, but I think about him every day. He worked for a prefab housing company, and most of the cabins on the property came from there. We started with the nine houses around the bandstand."

Piper needed to ask about her son. Though it seemed nosy and rude to interrogate this woman who had saved them from Dmitri and his minions, Sofia's safety was at stake. "How old is your son?"

"Seventeen." She dragged a hand through her spiky hair and averted her gaze. "He's a good kid. Plays the guitar and the banjo. Every weekend, he and his friends put on a show in the bandstand."

In a small voice, Piper asked, "Is Logan his name?"

Chris waved them toward the area under the second floor where a table with six chairs on each side stretched toward the floor-to-ceiling windows at the rear of the house. Moving quickly, she turned a corner and disappeared through a swinging door. "I'll make herbal tea. If you'd like something stronger, I've got a batch of home-made beer in the cellar."

"Just tea," Piper said as she entered the huge, efficient-looking kitchen with two stovetops and counters lined with a battalion of glass Mason jars used for pickling and canning. She had a lot more questions about the son but didn't want to push too hard and cause Chris to shut down. "Looks like you've been busy."

"We just finished putting together a couple hundred jars of salsa."

Apparently, the Offenbach Community Farm Project lived up to the name. "Do you sell your wares?"

"On a limited basis," Chris said. "We're more interested in developing a self-sustaining farm and garden. Several of the people who live here drive into Portland to work. Others are devoted full-time to the fields and livestock."

Gavin strolled into the kitchen and let the doors swing shut behind him. "What about Dmitri and his buddies?"

"You find a couple of rotten apples in every bushel." She set a glass teakettle on the burner. "I arranged for those three to live here while they rebuilt the chicken coop and repaired the barn. Their carpentry work is good, but their attitude stinks. Too hot-tempered. Dmitri keeps telling people—especially the teenaged boys—that he was in the KGB, but I don't think he's old enough. The KGB dissolved over twenty-five years ago, when Dmitri was only a toddler. And I've never heard him speak more than a few phrases of Russian."

"What's the point of making up a story like that?" Piper asked.

Gavin answered. "Makes him feel like a tough guy."

Chris took a loaf of zucchini bread from the fridge, set it on a plate and sliced off a few pieces. After she brought out cream cheese to go with it, Izzy made her presence known, nudging Chris's leg and giving a quiet but friendly sound. "Moof."

"Hungry?" Chris asked the mutt.

"Always." Piper took the collapsible bowl from her pack, filled it with water from the faucet and placed it on the floor.

Izzy took one slurp and stared longingly at Chris until she got a bite of the bread.

"I know the dog's name," Chris said. "How about you two?"

Piper introduced herself. "And this is Gavin Mc-Queen. He's a federal marshal."

"Aha, so Dmitri and his buddies were right."

"Not entirely," Gavin said. "I'm not here to arrest anybody or cause trouble. We're looking for a teenaged girl, and Izzy seems to think she's here in your house."

"Why are you looking for her?"

When his forehead crinkled and his lips thinned, Piper recognized Gavin's struggle to keep his WIT-SEC secrets. Lucky for them, she wasn't under similar constraints. "We need to talk to her about her father. He's been shot."

They heard a loud gasp from outside the kitchen. Sofia shoved through the swinging doors. "What do you mean he's been shot? Is he okay? OMG, Mc-Queen, why didn't you tell me?"

Chapter Five

The three females in the kitchen—four including Izzy—aimed poisonous glares at Gavin. Okay, maybe they were right and he should have leveled with Sofia during that first phone call. But she hadn't given him a chance to explain. And he wanted to control the direction of their conversation.

"Sorry," he said as he took out his cell phone. "Let me get an update on Marco's condition."

Sofia reached for his phone. "Give it to me. I'm the one who should talk to the doctor. I'm family."

His communications involved more than medical personnel. He'd also check with the guards from the US Marshals Service who were posted in the hospital. First of all, he'd talk to Beekman. "I'll take care of this."

"Why can't I do it?"

"The situation is complicated."

"The girl has a legitimate issue," Chris said. "You need to be honest with her."

Piper added her previously stated opinion. "I agree."

When in doubt, Gavin knew enough to change

the subject. "Here's a question for you, Chris. Why didn't you tell us Sofia was here?"

"You didn't ask."

Not yet. But that would have been his next question. "There's another reason. You wanted to protect her."

"You bet," she said adamantly. "She can stay here as long as she wants. Until I know what you're after, I won't turn her over to you."

"I feel the same way. Taking care of Sofia is my business. It's all that matters," he said. "Why does she want to hide from me?"

"Hello?" Sofia planted her fists on her hips and stuck out her chin, sending a ripple through her long, wavy black hair. "I'm standing right here. And I can answer my own questions. Ever since I was ten, people—especially you, McQueen—have been ordering me around. It's time for me to make my own decisions."

"But—"

"Stop." She held her palm in his face, but when he caught her gaze and stared back at her with furious intensity, she pulled back her hand as if she'd been burned. "Don't mean to be rude, but you've got to level with me. Is my dad all right."

He speed dialed the number for Inspector Marshal Beekman. "I need the most recent update on Marco Barbieri's condition."

"Last I heard, he's still in surgery," Beekman reported. "His bleeding is under control, and he's received transfusions. The doctors haven't elaborated on internal injuries. He'll be in ICU for a while. Won't be able to talk until late tomorrow at the earliest."

"Chances on recovery?"

"He's critical but expected to be okay."

"Keep me posted."

Before Gavin could end the call, Beekman added, "Here's another pertinent update. Tom Ivanov, the pilot and third member of the Dragon *troika*, escaped from prison in New Jersey. From all indications, he's headed toward the West Coast."

Gavin felt like he'd been punched in the gut. "Why is Ivanov coming this way?"

"To see his boss. Eleven months ago, Yuri Drako was transferred to the federal prison in Sheridan, Oregon."

Drako's presence so close to Marco and Sofia presented a clear, obvious threat. Gavin should have been informed. "Why is he here?"

"As you know, Drako has a dream team of attorneys who entered several pleas for a compassionate transfer until they found a judge to agree. Yuri Drako is in his nineties and near death. His son lives on the coast at Devil's Lake near Lincoln City."

"And his grandson?"

"That's correct."

Gavin recalled what Piper had told him. Marco claimed he'd been shot by "the grandson."

He ended his call with Beekman and turned to face the angry women. Even if he'd wanted to be gentle and sensitive, Gavin couldn't have pulled it off. He wasn't a great actor, and he'd been given some very bad news.

If necessary, he'd handcuff Sofia and drag her into protective custody. Ivanov had a well-deserved reputation as a stone-cold killer willing to sacrifice himself to further the cause. And Yuri Drako, the old dragon himself, lurked in the shadows nearby. Gavin knew what he must do.

"Your father," he said to Sofia, "is still in surgery. The doctors don't know the extent of his injuries, but he's expected to recover. No one is allowed to see him until late tomorrow or the next day, at which time I'll decide whether it's safe for you to go to the hospital."

Her anger faded. Tears glistened at the corners of her green eyes. "Are you sure he's going to be okay?"

"He's getting the best care possible and being guarded around the clock."

As a sob wrenched through her slender body, a young blond man joined her in the kitchen doorway. He wrapped Sofia in his embrace and held her as she wept against his shoulder. Both Piper and Chris looked on with empathy and concern. Izzy rubbed against Sofia's leg.

Gavin glanced toward Chris. "Your son?"

"Logan and Sofia have been dating since the end of summer. She started singing in the gazebo with his band every weekend. The girl has a wonderful voice."

Gavin remembered. When she was nine, Sofia had won a talent contest belting out the lyrics to "Let it Go" from the Disney movie *Frozen*. In WITSEC, he knew she'd be safer if she hid her talent. Someone outside the program might remember. The Dragon might recall a skinny child with long black hair who sang like an angel.

Gavin had advised her not to perform in public. As he gazed at the weeping teenager, he realized how futile his words had been. *Don't sing?* He might just as well ask the moon not to rise and the stars not to shine.

Could her performance be the way they'd found her and Marco? He doubted it. The idea that the Dragon's men had recognized Sofia from a sing-along at the commune seemed an unlikely coincidence. Turning toward Chris, he asked, "How many people usually attend your programs?"

"A couple hundred at the most, but the show is a viable way for musicians to promote themselves."

"How so?"

"Some of them are approached by producers who want to make demo tapes. Sofia and Logan had one of their songs recorded…" She hesitated. "The one from the Disney movie."

"'Let it Go,'" he said.

"That's the one." She couldn't help smiling. "One of their fans streamed their performance on some kind of online Tick-Tick or Tube Dube or some such. Everybody loved it. They went viral."

Inwardly, he groaned. Sofia's sweet soprano and delicate face had appeared all over the country. No surprise that one of the Dragon's men had showed up on the Barbieri doorstep. Had the shooter tracked her to the commune? Did he know about Logan? When he and Piper had driven here from Marco's house, had they been followed? Later, he'd deal with the multitude of questions. For right now, they needed action. "Let's get the hell out of here."

Still holding Sofia to his chest, the young man said, "I'm coming with you."

"No." Gavin was firm.

"But I can help. I'm a good shot."

"This is not a topic for discussion. I'm a federal marshal, and I give the orders. Sofia needs to be in protective custody immediately. You aren't tagging along."

Gavin's only decision was whether to call for backup, which would require them to wait, or to hit the road and get Sofia to safety. He opted for the latter. If Dmitri and his buddies were involved and had time to get organized, they might pose a threat.

"Logan and I can help," Chris said. "We'll provide cover until you get to your vehicle."

Izzy added a bark of support.

Gavin glanced from one to the other: the white-haired woman with a Remington rifle, her handsome young son, sweet Piper, who was becoming more appealing by the minute, her half-poodle truffle dog, and Sofia the songbird. Altogether, they made up one hell of a ragtag army. He needed to take charge before they came up with some sort of weird scheme. He asked, "Chris, do you have a truck?"

"In the attached garage."

"Perfect."

Gavin outlined the plan in wide strokes. Logan would drive while his mother rode shotgun, literally. The rest of them would hide in the back of the truck until they got to the front gate. He, Piper, Sofia and Izzy would jump into his SUV and go like the wind.

In the garage, Piper ducked inside the truck bed. "It smells like Chris was hauling goats in here."

"Entirely possible." He lowered himself to the cold metal floor of the Toyota pickup, leaned against the side and sprawled his long legs out in front of him. His Beretta nestled in his fist, he hoped he wouldn't need to use it.

"I like Chris," Piper said. "And I totally agree with the idea of becoming self-sustaining. This commune isn't a cult. It's an enclave of rational people in an increasingly irrational world."

"Is that something you learned at Wharton business school?"

She gave an annoyed snort that would have been obnoxious if it wasn't so damn cute. "Where are we headed?"

"Someplace safe."

"Can we stop at Marco's house so I can get my car?"

Gavin peered through the semidarkness in the garage at her heart-shaped face. If he hadn't been so frustrated and tense, he might have taken her in his arms, the way Logan had comforted Sofia. He would have told Piper the truth about how much danger they were in and how he'd take care of her. He would have stroked her auburn hair and kissed her forehead. None of those very natural actions was appropriate. One of the first rules in the US Marshals Service: don't get attached to the people you're protecting.

He looked away from her. "Forget your car. We can't make any stops."

Sofia clung to Izzy. Apparently, the teenager had stopped crying long enough to start feeling feisty. "This isn't my fault, you know. I can't help it if other people want to take pictures of me."

Were teenagers always so irresponsible and so... young? "We'll talk about this later. For now, stay down."

"Do you really, truly, think somebody is going to shoot at the truck?"

"Sofia," Piper snapped, "put a sock in it."

The automatic garage door squawked as it opened, and Logan hit the accelerator. The kid drove like a demolition derby champ, careening along the circular road toward the front gate and taking the curve on two wheels, which was quite a feat in a truck. Nothing else was moving. No cars or vans. Not even the goats scampered near the bandstand.

Just in case, Chris positioned herself with her long rifle sticking through the passenger's-side window. The LED streetlights glistened on her spiky white hair. At the latched gate, Gavin jumped from the rear of the truck to open it. Chris stood at his side, scanning in all directions for any approaching threat.

Logan drove through the opening, whipped a turn and slammed on the brakes to park beside the unmarked Ford Explorer. They rushed to take their positions: Gavin behind the steering wheel, Piper in the passenger seat, Izzy and Sofia in the back. Sofia put her window down and kissed Logan until Gavin put the SUV in Reverse and launched the vehicle onto the zigzag roads toward civilization.

He kept a close watch on the rearview mirrors. "I don't see anybody following."

"I'm looking," Sofia said. "There's nothing behind us but forest."

Beside him, Piper maneuvered so she could see into the back seat. "I guess Logan is your special guy. He's cute."

"Best friend," Sofia said. "We sound awesome when we sing together, but we're not serious, you know. Not unless my dad likes him."

Gavin had seen that passionate kiss before they'd parted and wasn't sure he believed her when she claimed they were only friends. Wouldn't be the first time she'd lied to him. "Keep watching for headlights."

"Duh, Marshal McQueen. Or maybe I should call you McPrincess."

She snickered at her own joke, and he let it slide. Long ago, he'd given up on demanding respect from Sofia. Better to have her snippy than depressed. "Just keep watching."

"What happens next? Are you going to stash me in some cheapo motel?"

His primary concern in finding a safe place was anonymity, which meant they wouldn't be booking

a deluxe room with a spa and a view. He also preferred easy access in case they needed to make a
quick change of location. "I have a place in mind."

"On a scale of one to ten, how scuzzy?"

"It's clean. That's all you need to know. We're not
on vacation."

"I have a suggestion," Piper said. "I know a little
hotel off US 5 near the Willamette River, and they
take dogs. We can get adjoining rooms."

"We'll see."

"It has WiFi, cable TV and a swimming pool,"
Piper said. "And 24/7 room service."

"Please," Sofia said. "Please, please, please."

For a moment, he considered handing the teenager
over to the FBI for safekeeping, but he'd developed a
relationship with both her and her father during the
past six years. Sofia might be an irritating smartass, but she was *his* smartass, and he couldn't help
feeling guilty about the current situation. Maybe he
should have monitored her more closely to be sure
she wasn't making demo tapes and appearing on
the internet.

Controlling her behavior was his job, and he'd
failed miserably. Her father had almost been killed,
and Sofia had developed a social media presence.
Gavin had not fulfilled his basic WITSEC respon-
sibilities.

He glanced toward Piper in the passenger seat.
Her steady gaze and calm demeanor told him that
she also believed in responsibility. She wouldn't want

him to dump Sofia with the FBI. "Fine," he said, "I'll consider your suggested motel."

Once again, he checked the rearview mirror. Nobody behind him. In spite of the danger that encircled them like an ever-tightening noose, they seemed to have made a clean getaway from the commune. After he had a chance to confer with his boss in Portland and make arrangements for Sofia and Marco to be relocated in a different WITSEC setting—somewhere far away from the Dragon—he'd be done with this case.

TAI DRAKO SLOUCHED in the passenger seat of the beat-up station wagon and peered into the dark forest through the dirty side window. He should have taken his Honda motorcycle. Sure, the souped-up Rebel made more noise than a car, but when Tai drove himself, he was in control. Right now, he was at the mercy of this Russian poser in grungy overalls.

Beside him in the driver's seat, Dmitri hunched over the steering wheel. Not a great driver, he scraped the passenger side of the car against a slender pine trunk and kept going.

"Why don't you turn on the headlights?" Tai asked.

"They'd know we're tailing them. Dumb question."

No dumber than following in the first place. What would they do when they caught up with the marshal? Tai wasn't equipped for a shoot-out. He'd left his Glock 13 and suppressor in Beaverton with that lady and her devil dog. The only reason he'd returned to the commune was to pick up another weapon. A waste of time and effort. Dmitri had given him a .25-caliber handgun—a lousy, little peashooter.

The gun shouldn't matter. Tai's part of the plan had never involved shooting or killing. He was supposed to find the girl, Sofia, abduct her and return to their hideout near his dad's house at Devil's Lake. Should have been easy, but everything had gone wrong. Instead of finding Sofia at home, her dad had answered the door in Beaverton. The old man had argued and shoved. Tai'd had to shoot him. He'd had to. There wasn't a choice.

"How long have you worked with the Dragon?" Dmitri asked.

"My grandfather?"

"Da, boychik. How many dragons do you know?"

He hated the way Dmitri used smatterings of Russian to make himself seem tough, which he definitely was not. "I met my grandpa when I was fifteen."

"In Jersey?"

"Yeah." That meeting had taken place almost ten years ago and the only thing Tai had gotten from it was the Yankees T-shirt he wore under his plaid shirt. The emaciated man with the wrinkled face and incongruous black hair hadn't impressed him. Tai preferred his grandparents on his mother's side, who were elders from the Siletz tribe and important executives in two casinos on the Oregon coast. The so-called Dragon had failed in his dumbass terrorist plan. Instead of being a powerful guy, he'd ended up in prison. Now Tai's father insisted that they risk everything to help Grandpa escape.

Tai scowled. Partnering up with Dmitri—a total loser—had been a bad idea. Tai needed to concentrate on the end goal, like he did when he played hockey. He ran his tongue over the partial denture that covered the gap in his front teeth. Forget teamwork. Grandpa might be a dragon, but Tai was a lone wolf.

On the winding road ahead, he glimpsed the Explorer's red taillights. "Slow down, Dmitri. You're too close."

"Don't tell me what to do."

"Just pointing out the obvious." He shot a glare at the jerkface. "Why didn't we put a tracer on the marshal's car? Then we could find him without following."

"I don't have that kind of equipment."

"You know, you can order that stuff online."

"We're fine," Dmitri said. "They'll never see us."

Tai heard loud baying from the dog who'd chased him away from the Barbieri house. His fingers tightened on the puny .25-caliber gun in his right hand. He wouldn't mind shooting that bitch.

Chapter Six

Piper unfastened her seat belt and reached between the front seats to pat the dog who continued to yowl. "That's enough, furball. Settle down."

Beside the dog, Sofia leaned over the back of her seat and stared through the rear window of the Ford Explorer. "Izzy is telling us to be alert, and she's right. In the moonlight, I can just barely see another car behind us. No headlights."

Holding back her fear, Piper squinted through the window. "I don't see anything."

Izzy threw back her head and gave a series of yips while Sofia chimed in. "Omigod, they're right behind us."

"Enough," Gavin said. "All of you sit down and fasten your seat belts, including Izzy."

Piper snapped an order. "Quiet, Izzy. Quiet now." To Sofia, she said, "In my backpack, you'll find a bag of doggy treats and a hippo chew toy."

"I know the one," Sofia said. "Happy Hippy."

As she refastened her seat belt, Piper swiveled her head toward Gavin, who seemed unperturbed. How could he stay so calm? She was freaking out, struggling to keep the panic out of her voice. "I thought we were in the clear."

"Not by a long shot."

His gaze focused on the rearview mirror as he deliberately slowed. What was he doing? The car behind them would catch up. "Why are you slowing?"

"Testing Izzy's and Sofia's vision." In less than five seconds, he pumped the accelerator. The tires caught and the Explorer lurched as they sped along on the twisting, narrow road. "They were right. I spotted the car."

On a sharp turn, she jostled against the passenger's-side window. Her pulse quickened. She'd gone from contemplating a room service order of cheeseburger and onion rings to a vivid memory of the thug who'd shot Marco. She remembered the gun, the knit cap, the Yankees T-shirt and the shooter's angry sneer that exposed a missing tooth. Was he in pursuit? "What are we going to do?"

Still paying attention to the road, Gavin spoke in a low, steady tone. "The guy driving the vehicle behind us is so familiar with this road that he doesn't need headlights. I'm guessing it's Dmitri or one of his pals."

"Is that good or bad?"

"Good because he's not very smart and we can outwit him."

"Right," she said.

"Or it could be bad because stupid people are unpredictable." Gavin frowned. "Anybody with two brain cells wouldn't do a chase on a single-lane road through a forest at night. They'd plant a tracer on the Explorer and find us when it was convenient. Our boy Dmitri might not be clever enough to use a tracking device or he might not understand how that simple technology works."

The dense forest began to thin and she knew they were approaching a more heavily trafficked road. She swallowed hard. "Are we going to be in a high-speed chase?"

"I need backup," he said. "By the time I summon the troops, it'll be too late. Instead, I'm going to return to Marco's house to meet up with the cops and marshals."

"How are you going to—"

"You'll see." He flipped switches on the center console and activated some kind of police radio. Then he told the person who answered that he was being followed by a suspect and needed assistance. He also said he'd be at the Barbieri home in less than ten minutes.

When Gavin looked in her direction, Piper tried to control her trembling. She didn't want to be scared and definitely didn't want him to know how truly frightened she was. Though she barely knew him, his opinion mattered.

"Brace yourself," he said.

Now what? Her fingers twisted in a knot. Her cheeks were on fire. Her breath came in hot, ragged gasps.

At the main road, Gavin swerved across one lane

and made a sharp left. Even though there were no other vehicles, it was a scary maneuver. He tapped other switches and punched buttons on the console of his unmarked vehicle. An array of red and blue lights flashed across the windshield visors, and—oh my God—her ears were hit by the squawking of a police siren.

From the back seat, Izzy barked in canine harmony with the siren. Sofia added her own garbled scream.

Piper closed her eyes, clapped her hands over her ears and tried to shut down her senses. The blast of noise and light had disoriented her.

How the hell did she get into this mess? During a normal day at her secluded cabin, the forest maintained a pleasant sameness that varied with the season but was always recognizable. The position of the sun gave her an idea of time. When the air smelled of rain, she knew to rush home. She heard nothing but birdsong, whispering wind in the tree boughs and woofs and growls from Izzy. A peaceful life, controlled but not boring.

She squinted at the highway stretched before them. The dotted line between the two lanes become a dizzying blur in the mist. Trees and shrubs beyond the glow of the headlights turned into a solid wall of dry autumn foliage, green pines and mossy branches. When the Explorer dodged around a slow-moving truck, she opened her eyes wider.

She felt Gavin's touch on her arm. Turning toward him, she dropped her hands so she could hear what he was saying over the noise of the siren and Izzy's howl.

"Are you all right?" he asked.

"Not at all, but thanks for asking."

He rewarded her with a reassuring smile—a contrast to his black leather jacket and the gun that never left his side. The odd combination worked for her. Gavin was tough but not a psycho. If she had to be in mortal danger, he'd be her first choice to protect her. In a tiny voice, she asked, "Did you lose him?"

"I don't see the other car in my rearview."

Then why was Izzy still making noise? "Please turn off the siren."

"Not yet," he said. "We'll be at Marco's house in just a few minutes."

While he continued to break speed limits, her eyelids slammed shut again. Talk about being in the wrong place at the wrong time. If she hadn't chosen this night to sell truffles to Marco, she wouldn't have been there when the shooter arrived. She could have avoided this whole terrible scene.

But if she hadn't been there, Marco might have bled to death. And Gavin wouldn't have located Sofia so quickly. Piper had served her purpose. She'd helped. And now she just wanted to go home. She rested her elbow on the center console and inclined toward him so he could hear what she was saying without her having to yell at him. "At Marco's house, I'm taking my car and driving back to my cabin."

He shook his head. "Not a chance."

"Why not?"

"You need to give a more detailed witness statement to the local police and talk to a sketch artist."

"I can do those things tomorrow."

"That's not the only reason, Piper. You said it yourself. When you saw the shooter, you became a witness. In danger."

Fighting hopeless tears, she objected. "He doesn't know my name, doesn't know where I live. I don't want to be part of this."

"There's a bright side." Without taking his eyes off the road, Gavin slipped his hand around her neck, pulled her closer and whispered, "We'll have a chance to get to know each other better."

In spite of a little thrill that tickled her spine, she pushed away from him. "I can't believe this. Are you flirting with me?"

"Absolutely not. I'm a pro, a marshal."

"And you have no human emotions."

"None."

Streetlights illuminated his annoyingly perfect profile. He was hot, no doubt about it. But not the right guy for her. No way would she get involved with a man who lied for a living. "This has to be the worst blind date ever."

At MARCO'S HOUSE, the array of vehicles had changed, but there were still several cars and a dark blue van labeled Crime Scene Unit. Though Piper couldn't remember any of their names, some of the local cops looked familiar. A tall, rugged-looking, blond guy with a five-pointed-star badge introduced himself as Deputy Marshal Dan Johnson. "Call me DJ."

Together, DJ and Gavin surrounded her, Sofia and Izzy, then rushed them into the house where other officers, attired in gloves and protective gear were processing the crime scene. Piper couldn't imagine how any clue would survive the number of officers and paramedics who had come before. On the way to the kitchen, she positioned herself so that Sofia would be shielded from the sight of her father's blood smeared in the entryway.

Gavin was less considerate and more direct. "Sofia, do you remember how I told you to always keep a backpack or small carry-on packed with your necessities?"

"My go-bag." She gave a quick nod. "It's in the front closet. I did like you said and got a boring color that wouldn't stand out."

"I'll get it."

"Thanks, Marshal."

Impressed with the teenager's calm attitude, Piper guessed that Sofia had done something like this before when she and her father had gone into WITSEC. A go-bag? Holding tightly to Izzy's leash, she turned to Gavin. "Is there anything I should do?"

"Get yourself a glass of water. Use the bathroom. Whatever." He shrugged. "We'll leave as soon as we're cleared."

"Cleared? What does that mean? I thought I was supposed to give a statement."

"Your safety comes first. First, an officer will check you ladies and Izzy for bugs and then—"

"Bugs? I assume you're not talking about ticks."

"Cute," he said without a smile.

"Who would plant a bug on me? I wasn't around anybody but Chris and Logan." When she met his gaze, she realized that she knew very little about the Offenbach mother and son. "Do you suspect them?"

"Not necessarily. Sofia was there for hours. She could have had contact with several people. Also, I've got to take your cell phone and any other electronic equipment."

"My truffles," Piper said. "I left my truffles in your Explorer."

"Your mushrooms aren't all that important, are they?"

"I need them back."

"Let's put this into perspective." She heard an edge of impatience in his tone. "Someone wants to kill you. That's the only thing that matters."

"Those truffles represent three afternoons' work. Marco already paid for them, and I don't feel right about giving him a refund. He'll want the goods."

"She's right," Sofia said. "He's probably got a whole meal planned around those truffles."

"If I have a chance," Gavin muttered, "I'll get them."

An officer wearing latex gloves came into the kitchen and used a machine attached to a wand, like a metal detector at the airport, to check them for bugs.

Even Izzy went through scanning. The same officer took their phones.

"When can I get my phone back?" Piper asked.

"You'll have to ask Marshal McQueen. He's in charge."

Feeling like she'd been put in her place, Piper sat at the kitchen table. On the counter near the sink, she noticed the mostly full bottle of pinot noir Marco had opened to toast her and Izzy. Only a few hours ago, that moment now seemed like part of the distant past. The chef had made a Russian toast—*nostrovia*—which seemed a little bit weird. She thought of another anomaly: the creepy man in overalls at the commune called himself Dmitri and claimed to be in the KGB. Was she sensing a thread? "Sofia, your dad is Italian, right?"

"As Italian as pizza, calzones and cannoli. He follows soccer, which he calls football, and goes to the opera. Can you believe it? Figaro, Figaro, Figaro. Dad is super Italian—the man bleeds red, white and green like the flag."

"Is he also part Russian?"

Sofia's eyes widened in surprise. "How did you find out? Nobody is supposed to know."

"Just guessing."

"Don't say anything to McQueen, okay? He'll think I told you."

He strode through the kitchen door carrying her blue-striped, insulated carrier with the truffles inside and a small gray suitcase. "Don't tell me what?"

"Nothing," Piper said as she grabbed the carrier

and took a look inside. Much to her relief, the truffles were unharmed.

He placed the go-bag on the floor at Sofia's feet. "Is there anything else you need from the house? We might not be coming back here for a long time."

"Are we moving again?"

"That's not my call."

"Not fair."

When she stood and stomped away from the table, Piper watched with concern. Sofia's shoulders had tensed and she'd wrapped her arms tightly around her middle as though trying to hold herself together.

"Here's the good news," Gavin said. "I made reservations at the place Piper suggested, the one that accepts dogs. When we get there, we can order from room service."

"Big whoop."

Though Sofia tried to sound snarky and above-it-all, her voice cracked. She was too young to be so bitter, and Piper ached for her. When she looked to Gavin, she saw a flicker of sadness in his chocolate-brown eyes. He didn't want to hurt Sofia, either. No doubt he regretted the way things had turned out and would rather see her happy instead of having her life torn apart. Again.

Piper gave him a nod. "I understand."

"Do you?"

"Yes." When they'd talked earlier, he'd as much as admitted to being lonely, and she knew why he felt that way. "Nobody likes to be the bad guy, but sometimes it's necessary. That's something I actually did learn at the Wharton School of Business."

Piper slung the strap for her insulated pack of truffles over her shoulder and followed him out the door, where she was herded into another unmarked SUV with heavily tinted windows. She sat in back with Izzy's head on her lap and Sofia beside her. Gavin took the passenger seat, and Marshal DJ was behind the wheel.

As they rode away from the house, she heard an undercurrent of male conversation from the front of the SUV as the two marshals discussed background checks on Dmitri and a pilot who was coming for them and the old dragon in federal prison at Sheridan. A pilot? A dragon? None of their talk made sense to her.

As they zipped along suburban streets, she reached over and touched Sofia's arm. "Are you okay?"

"Totally bummed," she said. "I'm sick of being a no-name girl with a nowhere life story. I hate, hate, hate all this hiding. How will I ever get to do anything important with my life if I can't be who I really am?"

Piper didn't know what to say. She couldn't encourage Sofia to tell her story to the world if it meant putting herself and her father in danger. "Have you talked to anyone about your past?"

"There was a therapist sanctioned by the Marshals Service, but I couldn't even tell her why we were in WITSEC. Nobody knows. Not even Logan, and I'm kind of falling in love with him."

Piper grinned. "I thought he wasn't a boyfriend."

"Well, maybe I changed my mind."

"Tell you what, Sofia. You can tell me about your past."

"Yeah?"

"I'm kind of a witness, too."

"I'd like that." Sofia grasped her hand and squeezed hard. "I'd like it a lot."

At the three-story hotel, Piper held Izzy's leash and allowed herself to be shuffled through a side door. She and Sofia had a room on the third floor with a not-so-stunning view of the parking lot. Gavin and DJ had the adjoining room.

Sitting at the end of the full-sized bed nearest the window, Piper kicked off her hiking boots, sprawled backward and groaned. "This is exhausting. How many times have you been spirited away in the middle of the night?"

"You get used to it," Sofia said. "On my first night away from home when I was ten, they had to give me something to help me sleep. Now, it's second nature."

Her young life had been intense, fraught with danger. Piper couldn't imagine how Sofia coped with losing her friends and her home. "Where did you live before you were ten? I know it was somewhere back East, but Marco never told me the exact location."

Sofia shrugged. "I'm not supposed to tell."

"Of course not," Piper said. "Sorry for asking."

"Jersey City." A huge smile stretched across her face, and she giggled as she recited her street address. "Omigod, you're the first person I've ever told."

Piper doubted that her complicity was a good thing, but she felt honored by Sofia's trust. "What did your house look like?"

"Red brick, two-story. I had my own bedroom, painted pink and mint green. Mama decorated it all, and she had super-good taste. Some parts of town were kind of awful, but our neighborhood was gorgeous. Lots of kids. We had a huge garden with a bird bath and a marble statue of St. Francis."

Thus far, Sofia hadn't said anything terribly incriminating, but Piper began to reconsider the wisdom of this conversation. They should talk to Gavin before Sofia revealed too much. "Are you sure you want to tell me about this?"

Sofia stalked across the room to the window and pulled the curtains closed. "Never supposed to leave a view into our room. There might be a guy out there in the darkness with a long-range rifle."

"Okay." Piper looked away, covering how shocked she was by the idea of a sniper. "Any other tips?"

"Sleep with your clothes on. We might have to run, and you won't have time to get dressed." Her smile returned. "This is all TMI, but it feels good to say it out loud. I haven't talked about my past with anybody but McQueen."

Piper wasn't sure she wanted the responsibility of knowing too much. "It's okay if you change your mind."

"There's no stopping me." Her grin was mischievous. "My dad's real name is Maxim Lombardi. He ran a *fantastico ristorante* with lots of pasta, veal scaloppine, eggplant Parmesan and—here's the weird part—beef stroganoff. That happened to be Yuri Drako's favorite."

"Drako?"

"The Dragon," Sofia said.

Chapter Seven

The hotel's large corner suite came equipped with a full-sized table, sitting area, kitchenette and two separate bedrooms on either side. Gavin draped his black leather jacket over the back of a chair and rolled up his sleeves. His tactical wristwatch showed the time: 1:37 a.m. Less than four hours ago, he'd entered Marco's home in Beaverton where he'd met Piper and her truffle dog. Though his primary goal—keeping Marco and Sofia safe—had been accomplished, he was far from satisfied. They were being threatened by a local shooter, and a notorious prison escapee was on his way across the country to Oregon.

DJ crossed the room, took a handful of evidence folders from a leather messenger bag and dropped them on the table. "Tell me about Piper," he said. "You're interested in her, aren't you?"

As a newlywed of three months, DJ pushed everybody else to couple-up.

"Sure, I'm interested in her. As a witness."

"Being married is great—expensive but great. You should try it."

"No thanks."

"I can tell you like Piper, and I don't blame you, man. She's pretty. Weird but pretty."

"Why weird?"

"No makeup. Her hair looks like she combed it with a tree branch, and she dresses like my twelve-year-old nephew. And truffles? What's up with that?"

"A gourmet thing." Though Gavin lived in Portland, which was one of the foodie capitals of the country, he'd never tasted a truffle and the supposedly fantastic smell reminded him of old gym socks. "She was selling those fancy mushrooms to Marco Barbieri when he was shot."

"Are you one hundred percent sure she's not involved in the attack?"

Gavin pointed to the folders. "Haven't you got a report from Beekman in there? He checked her out. Piper Comstock has no criminal record. She's somebody who happened to be in the wrong place at the wrong time. Innocent, but unlucky as hell."

"And now she's a witness. Are we going to turn her over to the FBI? Or get her into WITSEC?"

"We haven't talked about her options." Four hours didn't amount to much time when they'd been searching, chasing, and being chased. "First off, you and I have strategy to discuss."

"Starting with the dog." DJ shrugged his heavy shoulders. "Is there WITSEC for animals?"

"Izzy isn't a problem. When I give a command, she does it. No questions asked."

"Not like Piper."

Not hardly. The thought of Piper jumping to attention when he gave an order made him grin. This woman had backbone, character and a sense of humor—traits he found more appealing than mindless obedience. "I don't expect her—or anybody else for that matter—to follow my rules and do what I say. She's got a right to make her own decisions."

"Even if she's wrong?" DJ narrowed his pale blue eyes. The muscular, blond marshal had zero patience for witnesses who caused trouble. His talents leaned toward pursuit and apprehension rather than protection. "Does she understand how much danger she's in?"

"That's not the problem." He'd seen how scared she was when they were in the car chase. "She doesn't want to get involved."

"Sounds like you."

Gavin wanted to believe that he and Piper were on the same page. Occasionally, when her gaze met his, he saw a spark that made him think she might be interested in him, too. "For some reason, she thinks she can hop into her car, drive home and pretend this never happened. Doesn't believe the shooter will come after her."

"Denial." DJ selected a file from the stack and passed it to him. "There's a bunch of mug shots in here. If Piper identifies the person who attacked Marco and reads his rap sheet, she might wake up."

Gavin thumbed through photos of the Dragon's comrades in Jersey, his other family members and known associates. "After the attack, Marco mentioned the grandson. This might be a long shot, but does Yuri Drako have a grandson?"

"Yeah, he does." DJ nodded. "A young man in his twenties whose father married a Siletz woman whose family is a big deal in the tribal council and manages two casinos. The grandson's name is Taimar, which means 'thunder' in the language of the Blackfeet. He goes by Tai."

"Does Tai have a criminal record?"

"He's been picked up for a couple of dumbass teenager things. Drunk and disorderly. Disrupting the peace. Last year, he dropped out of college and tried out for the Seattle Kraken hockey team. Didn't make it."

Gavin held up a photo of a smiling young man with stringy black hair who was missing a front tooth. Typical hockey player. "This guy."

"That's him." DJ sat at the table. "Here's the part that doesn't make sense to me. The shooting in Beaverton didn't seem like a professional hit."

Gavin agreed. The shooter had been standing less than ten feet away when he pulled the trigger—too close to miss a kill shot. "Do we have an updated report on Marco's condition?"

"He's out of surgery. One bullet went through his upper chest near his shoulder. The other sliced through his gut. No vital organs were damaged, which means the shooter was either incompetent or had no intention of committing murder." DJ rested his elbows on the tabletop and unconsciously fiddled with his shiny, gold wedding band. "Also, he didn't shoot your girlfriend. Or her dog."

"You're right." The shooting didn't sound like an assassination. "Have you contacted Tai's father?"

"I wanted to talk to you first. Like you said…strategize."

There were a lot of pieces to this puzzle. The US Marshals Service—oldest branch of law enforcement in America—had several areas of responsibility. Not only did they run the long-term WITSEC program but they escorted convicted felons from one place to another and pursued wanted criminals. Gavin figured he had both hands full with protecting the Barbieri family and Piper. "Why don't you work with the local cops and investigate the shooter?"

"I'm on it," DJ said. "There's a marshal from Jersey who's tracking the escaped convict, Thomas Ivanov. The marshal's name is Esposito."

"I have a few choice words for him and the people he works with in Jersey," Gavin said, "starting with, 'Why the hell were Marco and Sofia placed in WITSEC so close to Drako's son and grandson?' Then I want to know why our office wasn't informed when the Dragon was transferred to the prison in Sheridan."

"Me, too. All I got when I questioned the Jersey office was a lame comment about how he's in his nineties and sick. Even on his deathbed, that old bastard is fierce."

"Can we interrogate him?"

"From what I understand, he's taken up permanent residence in the prison infirmary." DJ took a laptop from his messenger bag, flipped it open and logged on. "He's got a cozy setup with world-class docs, good drugs and cute nurses."

"The best money can buy," Gavin said. "Find out what it takes to arrange a face-to-face computer meet with Drako at the Sheridan prison."

"You got it."

"Also, set me up for a one-on-one with the hospital where Marco is laid up. As soon as the marshals guarding him are ready with video, let me know. Sofia needs to see her father."

"The local cops are on their way here to take Piper's statement and have her work with a sketch artist." DJ tapped away on his keyboard. "What should we do about Esposito?"

"We need to stay in touch with him." Though Gavin had every reason to be outraged with the lousy handling of important information by the marshals and the feds, he wasn't blameless. His failure to keep a close watch on Sofia while she made her presence known on social media might have resulted in the Dragon's crew pinpointing her location. Also, he reminded himself, the bureaucratic missteps that brought the Dragon to Marco's doorstep weren't Esposito's fault. Gavin exhaled a heavy sigh. "I'll make the call."

The time in Jersey was three hours later than on the coast, which meant it was nearly five o'clock in the morning. Inconvenient? *I hope so.* Rousing Esposito at the hairy crack of dawn gave him a nasty bit of satisfaction. He identified himself, "Marshal Gavin McQueen, Portland office."

"About time you called." Esposito didn't sound like a man who had been sound asleep. "You're WITSEC, right?"

"I'm the senior officer in charge of this case. My primary concern is the protection and safety of the witnesses."

"And a dog, right? Somehow, you got a dog involved."

There was no mistaking Esposito's smug, superior tone. The East Coast marshals liked to pretend they dealt with *real* crime, mobsters and high-powered felons while the rest of the service merely dabbled. Gavin wouldn't allow himself to be drawn into a spitting match. "What's the status on your escaped convict?"

"Ivanov." Esposito spoke the name as though it left a bad taste in his mouth. "He's vicious, smart and predatory. But I've got to give him props for smooth moves."

Gavin didn't need to hear about Ivanov's cleverness, and he didn't care about Esposito's opinion. "Do you have a location for him?"

"A reported sighting at an airfield in Ohio. That's where I'm headed right now."

"When you have confirmation, let me know."

Gavin ended the call. He wasn't looking forward to working with Esposito, but he'd do whatever necessary. They were on the same team, weren't they?

IN A BURST of energy, Sofia crossed from the hotel room window to the door and back again. In spite of her houndstooth leggings, scarlet lace-up shoes and purple puffer jacket, the long-legged, slender teen looked graceful and chic. Mesmerized, Piper watched the parade. She never understood how Sofia pulled off her color combinations and strange variations in eye shadow and lipstick—many of which were discordant but all of which worked. *This young woman was meant to be a star.*

Sofia's brow furrowed between her green eyes and she sucked her lower lip between her teeth before she paced again.

On her third route, Izzy joined the march, keeping pace with Sofia until she halted in front of the television set. "Do you know what's ironic?"

"Tell me," Piper said.

"I'm not sure I'm using the word correctly. Does 'irony' mean sarcastic or something that's the opposite of what you'd expect?"

"Close enough."

"Mr. Drako located my family because of my media presence, but he's the one who got me started singing in public. Ironic, huh?"

"Correct."

"One night when I was helping out at the restaurant, I started humming to myself. Drako overheard and asked me to sing." She whipped off her polka dot bucket hat and shook her head so her long black hair tumbled around her shoulders. "It was that kind of restaurant. There was an upright piano in the corner and a guy who played the violin. Sooner or later, somebody would get up and launch into an aria or a show tune. It didn't take much encouragement to get me to show off. No surprise, huh?"

Piper was the opposite. Though she had a decent voice and had taken years of guitar lessons, she hated performing. "Did he ask you personally?"

"You bet. He was a strange old guy with a dark tan and a million wrinkles. His black hair, combed straight back from his forehead, didn't have a single trace of gray. Usually, he and his two buddies— they called themselves the *troika*—talked in Russian, but Mr. Drako was okay with English. He told me I was a pretty girl. A *devushka* or something like that. I never learned the language, but my dad grew up speaking Russian with his mom, my *babushka*."

"That's the Russian part of your family," Piper said.

"Russian, Polish, whatever. *Babushka* used to sing me a lullaby, 'Bayushki Bayu.' I thought Drako would want me to sing that song but I didn't know the words very well, and I loved 'Let it Go' from *Frozen*. I won a talent contest when I was nine singing that song." She reached down to pat Izzy, the fan-dog, who attentively observed her every move. "The video of me singing that song is the one that got picked up on social media and went viral."

"Drako liked it?"

"Every time he and his guys came in for dinner, he asked me to sing. He'd listen and close his mid-night-black eyes and tell me how I ought to be on Broadway. Hard to believe he's a bad guy. But he is. Really bad." She frowned. "Marshal McQueen always warned me about singing in public. I should have paid more attention."

Piper's heart ached for this clever young woman whose survival depended on hiding her talent. There had to be a way around this obstacle. "If I'm going to understand how you and your dad ended up in WITSEC, I need to know more about the *troika*."

"They didn't know dad spoke Russian. While he served them Stroganov, borscht and blintzes that he learned how to cook from his mother, he picked up bits of their conversation."

Piper easily imagined the scene. A busy restaurant, serving mainly Italian food, where Marco played host and tried to keep everybody happy. "Go on."

Sofia exhaled a heavy sigh, peeled off her puffer jacket and plopped down on her bed. "This is where I should explain something important about my family. It happened when I was five years old and changed everything. More important than going into WITSEC, more than winning song contests, even more important than the first time Logan kissed me. It was the day my mother died."

"I'm sorry," Piper said. This young woman had experienced more than her share of tragedy in her sixteen years. "If you don't want to, you don't have to talk about it."

"Mom's death was one thing I could tell the shrink about. We covered the trauma again and again and again. She told me that I'd never recover from the loss, but I could learn to accept it. Not like my dad."

Piper had seen the endless sorrow in Marco's eyes and had heard the pain in his voice when he'd spoken of his late wife. "Her name was Gina."

"He was supposed to call her Angelica, but he sometimes forgot." She welcomed Izzy beside her on the bed. "And he wasn't supposed to have photos of her, but he did. All over the house, there were pictures hidden. Tucked inside their favorite book of poetry or hidden under the base of a lamp."

Erasing the past seemed so cruel. "He must have loved her very much."

"She was his whole life. It totally destroyed him when she was shot in cold blood during a bodega robbery in Manhattan. NYPD couldn't find a motive, called it an act of senseless violence. As if that makes it all right? I hate the guy who did it. He was never caught or charged or arrested."

Such an injustice could deeply affect a person and change the course of her life. Piper's personal tragedies—losing her job and divorcing her cheating husband—felt minor in comparison. "Seems like your therapist gave you some decent advice. How did your dad react?"

"Threw himself into work and kept really, really busy. I tried to console him. But what did I know? I was a kid." She propped herself up on her elbow. "After Mom's death, my dad hated criminals, especially those who got away with illegal stuff. When he overheard what Drako was planning with his *troika*, he couldn't turn his back and walk away. He had to stop them before innocent bystanders were murdered."

Sofia's unspoken tension affected her. Piper's pulse went into high gear, and she felt the drumbeat of surging blood throughout her body. Something bad was coming, something bigger than she could have imagined. "What was the plot?"

"The *troika* was planning a domestic terrorist action at the airport in Newark. We studied 9/11 in school, so I knew what terrorism meant. When Dad explained, he simplified so I could understand. One of the guys in the *troika* was a pilot, and his part in the scheme was to hijack a plane. Innocent people would be taken hostage, hundreds of them. They could all be killed unless my dad told the authorities."

Piper never expected to hear about a grandiose plot like this. She took a moment to absorb the gravity of the proposed crime as well as the personal implication for a ten-year-old girl who had lost her mother to senseless violence.

Sofia continued. "He told me he had to report the *troika*'s plot to the FBI, and we might have to go into witness protection, leave our home and our friends. It was a lot to ask."

"But you agreed," Piper said.

"How could I say no?" Her green eyes swamped with tears. "We had to stop Mr. Drako and the *troika*. For Mama's sake."

A brisk tap on the door from the adjoining bedroom startled Piper. She'd been so absorbed by

Sofia's story that reality had faded away. What could she do to help this young woman? How to protect her?

Gavin called her name. "Room service, ladies. Open up."

Sofia whispered, "Don't tell McQueen about this. He'll be really mad."

"But he already knows about Drako and the plot."

"Yeah." Sofia dashed the tears from her cheeks. "He doesn't know I've told you. I'm not supposed to talk to anybody about my past. Please, don't tell him."

Was she supposed to lie, look Gavin in the eye and lie to him? In normal circumstances, she had no problem keeping secrets. But Sofia's story went far beyond normal. Piper wanted to help the teen but the events of her past were too complicated for her to handle. If she talked to Gavin, he might know what to do. But there was no way Piper could betray Sofia. "You can trust me."

When she opened the door between rooms, her gaze alighted on Gavin's face. His slight frown seemed suspicious and judgmental. "What took you so long?"

A dozen lame excuses fluttered through her mind. Really not good at lying, she looked away from him. Maybe she'd only imagined his guarded attitude. Her guilt might be making her nervous. In a halting voice, she said, "Come in."

He pushed a rolling cart laden with grilled cheeseburgers and onion rings. The smell punched Piper in the gut. She'd been hungry. Now the thought of eating made her sick. If she didn't step away, she'd probably throw up and make everything else worse.

"Excuse me." She pivoted, dashed to the bathroom and closed the door.

Chapter Eight

Wagging her tail and rubbing her head against his thigh, Izzy greeted Gavin and his cart of food. Forty-five minutes ago when they'd arrived at the hotel, both Piper and Sofia had demanded room service, but now Piper was hiding in the bathroom and Sofia regarded him with a weird expression—a combination of panic and rage. Either she was ready to burst into tears or to tell him, in no uncertain terms, what a horse's ass he was. Clearly, something had gone wrong, and he needed to figure out what the hell it was.

He reached down and scratched between Izzy's ears. At least the dog was happy to see him. Since this hotel catered to the canine trade, he'd been able to order a portion of kibble along with the post-midnight snack of burgers. Gavin placed the dog food and a bowl of water on the tiled floor outside the bathroom. Then he turned to Sofia. "I thought you were starving."

"Thanks, McQueen." She uncoiled her long legs, took her plate to the table and sucked down a slurp of vanilla milkshake through a straw. "Did you get anything for yourself besides coffee?"

She knew him too well. He picked up his coffee mug from the tray and replied, "You know how much I love my caffeine."

"You're an addict. You know that, don't you?"

For a moment, he sat quietly at the table and watched her inhale the burger and onion rings. Sofia wasn't one of those teenaged girls who existed on a lettuce leaf and air. She had a healthy appetite for everything, including pasta, which pleased her father who tested some of his recipes with her. *Was she ready to see her dad?* Gavin had arranged with the marshals who were guarding Marco at the hospital to set up a live video feed on a computer tablet. Right now, Sofia's dad was unconscious, resting quietly in ICU after surgery, and expected to make a full recovery.

Though the prognosis leaned toward good news, Gavin expected Sofia to be upset when she saw him in a hospital bed. No matter how much she moaned and groaned about her father making unreasonable curfews and not understanding about her special boyfriend, she loved her dad. He was her only family, all she had left.

He sipped his black coffee. "Nice hotel, huh?"

"Way better than the dump you took us to last time." Two years ago, there had been a false alarm when classified info had been compromised. Many of the West Coast witnesses had been moved to more secure locations. "Dis. Gus. Ting."

At times like this, he missed ten-year-old Sofia with her gentle voice and innocent eyes. "You were only there for three days."

"And I missed a biology test," she said as though it had been the end of the world.

Marco had needed to fake an excuse for her. He couldn't come right out and say that his daughter would miss class due to an FBI breach and encroaching danger from domestic terrorists. "The teacher let you make it up."

"Only because you came to my school, pretended to be a visiting relative and dazzled her with your sneaky smiles and your black leather jacket."

"Yeah? You think I'm dazzling?"

"Get over yourself, McQueen. I'm just saying, I got an A-plus in biology."

The door to the bathroom opened and Piper stepped out. She'd taken the time to splash water on her face and run a comb through her wavy, shoulder-length, auburn hair. Not much of a makeover, but he liked the fresh, clean way she looked. Avoiding his gaze, she said, "We need toothpaste."

"Are you okay?"

"Sorry for running away from you." She patted Izzy's curly head. "I guess the stress of the day caught up with me. In addition to toothpaste, I've got to get a change of clothes. I borrowed this sweatshirt from Sofia, and I'm getting it all sweaty."

"Maybe she'll let you borrow something else."

Piper shook her head, and her curly hair ruffled

softly around her face. "That won't work. She's a size two, and I'm Godzilla."

He would have called her body nearly perfect— slender with just the right amount of curves. But Gavin knew better than to discuss clothing sizes with women. "We'll find something for you to wear tomorrow."

"No problem. I'll be back at my cabin tomorrow."

Seriously? Did she really intend to ignore all the danger signs? "We'll see."

When she joined them at the table, Gavin rose and pulled out her chair for her as if they were sitting down to a gourmet dinner in a fine restaurant. From the corner of his eye, he noticed Sofia watching him and hoped she wouldn't say anything sarcastic about the gentlemanly way he treated Piper.

Before Sofia could blurt out a snarky comment, he deflected. "Your dad came through surgery with flying colors. He's going to be fine."

"Are you sure about that?"

He took the eleven-inch computer tablet from the second shelf of the rolling cart and activated the screen. An image appeared, showing a hospital room where Marco lay motionless on the bed, a white bandage on his shoulder, IVs in his arms and a breathing apparatus that covered his mouth and nose. A nurse in dark blue scrubs checked the readings from several machines that monitored his condition.

Sofia grasped the edges and held the screen close to her face as though she could dive inside and join her dad. "I should be there. I want to be with him."

"Tomorrow," Gavin promised, "after he wakes up."

Piper peeked at the tablet. "He looks good, and he's being well cared for."

"I should be there," Sofia repeated.

The tremor in her voice reminded him of when she was a vulnerable ten-year-old. Gently, he rested his hand on her shoulder. "As soon as the doctors say it's okay, I'll take you to him."

"This is so wrong, McQueen. Why? Why did the Dragon have to hurt him?"

He shot her a warning glance then looked toward Piper. "This isn't something we can discuss. You know that, Sofia."

"Well, excuse me." The innocent child was replaced by the angry teenager. "Criminals tried to kill my father, and you're telling me to back off. As if I can't handle it? Come on, McQueen."

"We're investigating." He turned toward Piper. "In just a few minutes, the local police are going to be here with a sketch artist. They'll want to talk to you, so I need for you to come into the other room. Dig into that burger."

Sofia held her hamburger in one hand and the tablet in the other while Piper took a ladylike nibble of her onion rings. As he watched them, Gavin realized that he hadn't come close to figuring out the off-key attitude he'd sensed when he'd first entered the room. When he left the table and sat on the edge of the bed, Izzy joined him. If the dog could talk, she would have kept him informed.

Sofia scowled and licked ketchup off her finger. "Do I have to talk to the cops?"

"They'll have a few questions." A touchy subject; her boyfriend and others at the commune would be considered suspects. Since the local police didn't know about the witness protection issues, they'd look for the shooter among friends and associates of Sofia and her father. "After the police are done taking Piper's statement, I'll bring you into the room. Shouldn't be a problem."

"Yeah, yeah, I know the drill." She returned to her bed, still staring into the screen. "I'm keeping this tablet, McQueen."

"Absolutely." He'd expected that demand and had disabled the connections to cell phones and WiFi. If Sofia had access to the internet, she'd surely use it and get herself into trouble. "The tablet only has one channel. Only the connection to the hospital. So don't go messing around with the settings."

Her eyes narrowed when she looked at Piper. "McQueen doesn't want me to have contact with anybody else. It's like I'm a prisoner."

Piper met her gaze. "We should try to cooperate."

"Ha! You don't know him like I do."

The two women seemed to be communicating in code, and he'd had enough of it. Sofia had made it crystal-clear that she wouldn't work with him. Possibly, he'd have better luck with Piper if he could get her alone. He went to the door between the two rooms. "Piper, bring your burger and come with me. Sofia, you stay here until I let you know that the cops are ready to take your statement. If you need anything, inform the marshal posted in the hallway."

"A guard?" She bit her lower lip. "I can't believe you have a guard outside my room."

"For your protection."

He refused to launch into an argument he'd never win. In a few quick moves, he whipped the room service cart back into the suite he shared with DJ and closed the door behind Piper and Izzy, who was glued to her side.

He guided Piper to the large table, set her hamburger, which she'd barely tasted, in front of her chair and filled a mug from the thermal coffeepot in the kitchenette—not particularly tasty but at least it was hot. No one else was in the room, and he intended to take advantage of these moments alone with her.

"Okay," he said. "What's going on between you and Sofia?"

IGNORING HER BURGER and onion rings, Piper took a sip of the steaming liquid and gazed down into the mug. "Clouds in my coffee," she murmured.

"What are you talking about?"

"It's a line from an old Carly Simon song about dreams being clouds in your coffee, reflections that are hard to read."

She looked up at him and saw confusion in his dark brown eyes, which was understandable after her odd comment. But how could she tell him the straightforward, unvarnished truth? Not only had she promised Sofia to keep her secrets, Piper had been having complicated, inappropriate thoughts about Gavin. She was drawn to him, and a little afraid of him, and resentful. And, most of all, cautious. As much as he claimed to be a protector, this man wielded the undeniable power to hurt her.

He'd rolled up his shirtsleeves, and she noticed his strong, capable hands and the black hair sprinkled on his forearms. Too easily, she imagined him stroking her cheek and gliding his fingers lower to her throat and her shoulders. Though she had no reason to expect him to touch her, she sensed a similar attraction from him.

"Piper," he said, calling her back to the reality of hot coffee and a hotel room suite, "what were you and Sofia talking about before I came into the room?"

From what she knew, his job as a federal marshal required him to ask nosy questions and make unreasonable demands. He'd told her that he lied for a living, but she had no obligation to do the same. Piper looked him in the eye and spoke the truth. "I promised Sofia that I wouldn't tell you."

He held her gaze for several seconds. "You should reconsider."

"I won't change my mind," she said. "She trusts me, and I can't betray her."

Gavin bolted to his feet. His abrupt move disturbed Izzy, who also leaped to her feet and gave a rumbling growl deep in her throat. The dog looked from Piper to Gavin and back again, unsure of which side to take.

On the opposite side of the table, Gavin paced.

The limited space in the hotel room suite closed around them, and she tilted back in her chair to create more separation. "I can understand Sofia," he said. "She gets obstinate and unreasonable. She's sixteen, full of angst and hormones. But you're an adult."

"That's a little bit condescending."

He rested both palms down on the table and leaned closer. "I want to protect you, both of you and Izzy, too. But I can't do my job while you're playing hide-and-seek with me."

"This isn't a game." She rose to face him. "I'm not going to lie to you, Gavin. You might not like the truth, but here it is. Sofia and I had a private conversation, and I refuse to tell you what it was about."

"Since you're such a big fan of truth, here are a couple of real-life facts. We don't assign people to WITSEC unless the danger is real. Sofia has been under mortal threat for the last six years. People want to kill her and Marco. Tonight, her father was almost murdered."

"I know. I was there."

"Then, there's you. You're a witness, which means the shooter has motive to kill you."

"I'm aware of the danger. The shooter didn't attack me right away, but it doesn't mean he won't come after me later. I know that's a possibility."

"Do you? You seem to think you and Izzy will go skipping back to your cabin without a care. No harm done. That won't happen."

"You can't be sure."

"I'm a federal marshal, a trained professional

with access to detailed computer intel and foren-sics. Posted in my office is a photo array of the Ten Most Wanted Fugitives. Keep me in the loop, Piper. Whatever secrets you're holding might be the key that leads to the man who shot Marco and prevents further violence, including an attack on you."

Though he sounded reasonable, his intensity amped, and she responded to his barely contained anger. Her heart pumped faster, and it was difficult to draw breath. Using every bit of her self-control, she lowered herself into her chair at the table. When she tried to lift her coffee mug, her hand trembled too much. Instead, she picked up a fork and speared an onion ring. "I have nothing more to say."

"Simple question," he said. "Were you and Sofia discussing her boyfriend?"

Relief washed through her. No problem with this topic. "We weren't talking about Logan."

"What about anyone else at the commune?" he asked. "Like Dmitri and his pals. Or even Chris Of-fenbach."

"Not Logan's mother." The spunky woman with spiked hair wouldn't have had time to get in posi-tion for a car chase. "How could you suspect her?"

He raised an eyebrow, changing his appearance from hostile to inquisitive. "We've got to consider all aspects."

Piper noted how he cleverly included her in his investigation by saying "we." When she'd worked in the corporate world, she had extensively used interrogation tactics. If he expected her to crumble, he had another think coming.

Calmly, she dipped her onion ring in ketchup and took a salty bite. As long as Gavin concentrated on the commune, the secrets of Sofia's past were safe. "Since a car chased us when we left the commune, it makes sense that the shooter would be someone who lived there. I'm thinking of Dmitri and his pals."

He sat opposite her at the table. His attitude morphed from outrage to something more cordial. Was it a trap? Was he trying to lull her into a false sense of security so she'd get careless about what she said?

"It would really help," he said, "if you could tell me any other names that Sofia mentioned. Maybe somebody who worked with her father. Or a friend from school. She's close to you. She trusts you, right?"

In negotiation, it wasn't wise to volunteer new information. Therefore, she carefully edited her comment. "Sofia has visited me at my cabin several times. She feels safe there."

"Did she ever tell you what she was afraid of?"

Piper realized that she'd said too much. Time to shut down and redirect the conversation. She tossed an onion ring to Izzy, who caught it midair. The mutt loved people food. "Moof," Izzy said.

"We chatted about teenage stuff," Piper said. "Arguments she'd had with friends. Possible boyfriends."

"Like Logan?"

"He was mentioned. She claimed he was special but not her boyfriend." Absolutely true. Sofia told her about a boy whose family lived at the commune. She'd suspected her father wouldn't approve. "Of course, she didn't like her father's curfews and rules."

Gavin smiled and his gaze softened. Though she noted the very pleasant change in his expression, she didn't allow herself to be fooled. She recognized the game he was playing, trying to catch her off guard. "Sofia is a typical teen," he said. "She needs boundaries."

"Agreed."

"Did she talk about her mother? What would her mom think of Logan?"

Piper knew her expression had changed when he spoke of Sofia's mother. The story of her tragic death had had an impact. Determined not to betray the teen, Piper hoisted her burger to cover her mouth. But her eyelids blinked.

Gavin sharpened his focus on her. He must have guessed that he'd struck pay dirt. "Did Sofia tell you what happened to her mother?"

No way could Piper answer without lying or telling him what Sofia had said about her past and how she'd gotten into WITSEC. Silence offered the only out. Piper took a massive bite of the hamburger and filled her mouth, chewing vigorously and barely noticing the taste.

In a persuasive voice, he asked, "Have you ever heard the name Drako?"

Trouble, trouble, trouble. He'd pried open the lid

to Pandora's box, and she'd be forced to reveal everything Sofia had told her in confidence. How had she allowed this to happen? Obviously, her negotiating skills had grown rusty from disuse.

Gavin persisted. "What about Taimar Drako? His name means 'thunder.' He's from Devil's Lake."

The door to the suite opened wide. Marshal Johnson and three plainclothes police entered. Izzy greeted them all, and Piper swallowed. She needed to bring herself under control before she made a huge mistake.

Chapter Nine

After her verbal sparring match with Gavin—a face-off that he had nearly won—Piper's interview with the local plainclothes police felt as tame as a friendly chat at a church social. The detectives asked questions and she answered truthfully. Midway through the conversation, they all paused to admire her description of Izzy's heroic attack on the shooter. While the curly-haired mutt preened and offered her snout for pets and treats, Piper glanced up and noticed Gavin watching her with a dark, steady, unreadable gaze that sent a shiver across her shoulders.

One of her best skills when she'd worked in PR and marketing involved intuition—not the sort of goopy clairvoyance her auntie in Atlanta used for match-making but a sharp perception about what would happen next. When she'd been fired, she'd known her boss's intention as soon as she'd looked him in his piggish little eyes. Before she had actual proof of her husband's cheating, she'd sensed his infidelity. Continued deception had twisted his grin into a sneer and caused his hands to tremble. In him, she'd recognized the grotesque face of a liar, a scumbag. When it came to Gavin, she had none of those negative impressions—maybe because he was lying to her for the right reasons.

The primary detective from Beaverton sat at the head of the table, beside her. Tapping his pencil on a paper tablet, he asked, "When Marco mentioned a grandson, did he use a last name?"

"No." But Gavin had dug deeper. He'd asked her about Taimar Drako.

"Did Marco say anything else to identify the shooter?"

"Sorry, but no."

"When the shooter ran, did you see his vehicle?"

"I heard a motorcycle starting up," she said. "When I arrived earlier, I hadn't seen one."

"My forensics team took imprints from motorcycle tires in the yard by the driveway." The detective glanced toward Gavin. "My guess? It's something like a Honda Rebel."

Gavin nodded but said nothing. When she'd first met him, she'd lumped him into a lawman category that included mostly decent men and women who dedicated their lives to helping and protecting others. Piper had seen him as a federal marshal with the potential of being something more—a friend, a confidant or even a lover. Then he'd told her about the lying inherent in his work, and she'd gotten confused. He'd as much as told her that she'd be a fool to trust him, but he'd also saved her life in the car chase and sincerely cared for Sofia and Marco. Izzy adored him. To make things even more complicated, she recognized an undeniable thread of attraction woven between them and pulling her closer.

Of course, she'd never betray Sofia, but she very much wanted to level with Gavin. Piper knew that Sofia only had part of the story. The teenager knew about the long-ago crimes, but the teenager had only been ten years old at the time. She wasn't aware of the current developments and dangers.

Gavin had the whole story. If only Piper could have an honest, open conversation with him, she might be able to help figure out what was happening.

When the local police detective completed his interview, he directed her to a plain, padded chair beside a desk in a quiet corner of the suite by the curtained window and introduced her to Vincent Winston, a freelancer who often worked as a sketch artist for the Beaverton and Portland police. The young man shook her hand and took a seat at the desk where a blank computer screen reflected the room.

Gavin joined them and greeted Winston. "Mind if I watch?" he asked.

"Not a problem, Marshal McQueen." Winston's full lips pulled into a wide grin beneath his scraggly mustache. His narrow face seemed too thin for his large features, especially his saucer-sized brown eyes, and ears that stuck out like cup handles.

"We've worked together before," Gavin told Piper. "Winston is a pretty good portrait artist when he's not doing forensics for the police."

"Nice compliment."

"I mean it," Gavin said. "A few minutes ago, I saw you sketching. Will you show Piper what you drew on your pad?"

With a flourish, Winston flipped a couple of blank pages and displayed a pencil drawing of Izzy with her head cocked and an inquisitive gleam in her eyes. "Couldn't help myself," he said. "She's a star."

"This is fantastic." Piper took the pad from him and studied it. "In just a few pencil strokes, you caught her attitude of curiosity and intelligence."

"That's what Winston does best," Gavin explained. "All the forensic facial imaging software in the world can't duplicate his ability to illustrate emotion. Now, I'm going to shut up, sit back and let the artist do his job."

"You can keep the sketch of your dog," Winston said.

"Only if you sign it."

He scrawled his signature in the lower right corner and tore out the sheet of paper. "Let's get started. I heard you talking to the detective, so I've got a pretty good idea of what happened. I want you to concentrate on the shooter. Close your eyes and visualize him in your mind. Okay? Tell me your impressions. What's the first thing you see?"

"A huge, black gun. I guess it has a silencer. The guy holding the grip has strong hands and wrists. He's average height, wiry but not skinny. The muscles and tendons in his neck are tense. Breathing hard, his complexion is ruddy, and he's nervous."

"Why nervous?"

She shrugged. "Like he made a mistake or something. Or maybe he's worried about Izzy. Some people are scared of dogs."

"Moof," Izzy said, almost as though she was scoffing.

"What else?"

She pointed to her mouth. "He's missing a tooth on the left front side."

"Hair color?"

"Brownish. He's wearing a black knit cap, so I can't tell you how it's cut. His eyes are deep brown, and he has thick, black eyebrows, like yours. He seems really angry. And very young, too young to be a killer." She shook her head. "That's all I can remember."

"How about facial hair?"

"I didn't notice anything." She avoided making a comparison with the artist's sad little mustache. "The shooter was clean-shaven."

"You must have been scared."

"You'd think so," she said. "But at the time, I wasn't aware of how I felt. Now that the threat has passed, I'm terrified."

Beside her, Gavin spoke quietly. "You're right to be worried, but you're dead wrong about the danger being gone. Don't kid yourself, Piper. You're a witness. He'll come after you."

"Or not," she said. "Maybe he wasn't supposed to shoot me or Marco. Maybe he had a different agenda."

"Such as?"

"He could have come to Marco's house to threaten him. Or even to kidnap him."

Gavin nodded. "That's a good thought."

"I have my moments." Even if he was correct about the threat from the shooter, there wasn't much more she could do to protect herself. She'd already turned herself over to his care. "Please don't interrupt. I'm trying to concentrate. Winston, is there anything else?"

Without showing her the sketch, the artist asked for other details: the shape of his face, his jawline, cheekbones and ears. "Any tattoos? Visible scars?"

A memory popped into her mind. "He had a tat on his right wrist. I'm not sure what it was." She looked over her shoulder. "I should tell the detective. I hadn't remembered the tattoo until just this minute."

"I'll let him know," Winston said. "Now, I want you to slow down. Inhale for four seconds, exhale for six. Close your eyes again and think about the tat."

Piper understood his instructions. She regularly practiced yoga and was familiar with deep breathing exercises that encouraged meditation. In her mind, she recalled the moment when Izzy charged the shooter. His arms flailed, giving her a clear view of the tattoo. "A jagged black thunderbolt."

She traced the design on the back of her wrist, recalling that Gavin had asked about a man whose name meant thunder. She glanced toward him, looking for confirmation, but he said nothing.

"Okay, Piper." Winston turned his rough sketch toward her. "Is this the guy?"

The gifted artist had caught the attitude of the shooter who seemed hostile but young and uncertain at the same time. Piper wasn't sure how Winston had created the portrait, but she saw tension in the shooter's mouth and the fear in the tilt of his head. "The resemblance is amazing, but I think his eyes were closer together and turned down at the edges."

Winston flicked a switch and turned on his computer. "Give me a couple of minutes to set up. My sketch gives us a starting point. Then I'll use imaging software to fine-tune."

Leaning back in her chair, she sipped her lukewarm coffee and swirled it around in her mouth before swallowing. Tasted flat and somehow gritty, but the session with Winston made her feel like she'd helped the investigation. If Gavin would open up to her, she might be even more useful. She gave him a nudge. "You mentioned somebody named Taimar whose name means thunder. Could that explain the lightning bolt tattoo?"

"It's possible."

"Maybe if you showed me his photo, I could identify him." That seemed to be SOP in police shows she watched on TV and movies. "Don't they call it a photo array?"

"Does that happen on *Law and Order*?"

"Am I wrong?"

"Not at all." He rubbed his eyes, and she wondered if he was as tired as she was. "But I don't want to show you any pictures until after you're done with the sketch artist. You might zoom in on a photo for the wrong reason and misidentify the shooter."

"That missing tooth makes him stand out."

"And what if I showed you six photos of men with missing teeth?"

"Point taken."

Beneath her chair, Izzy had dropped her head onto her front paws and fallen asleep. In spite of the caffeine she'd been drinking, Piper felt the same. It was after two thirty. Today had been exhausting, and she suspected tomorrow would be just as bad. "Before I go to sleep tonight, I need to take Izzy for a walk."

"I'll do it." Gavin stood, pushed back his chair and patted the dog on her head. "Let's go, girl. Ready for a stroll?"

When Izzy looked to Piper for instructions, her loyalty was gratifying. The mutt liked Gavin, that went without saying, but Piper still ranked as the alpha in their unit. She rewarded Izzy with a smile. "You can go with him. He's a nice guy who carries a Beretta in case you run into trouble. You can trust him."

Gavin slipped into his black leather jacket. "That might be the nicest thing you've said about me."

"Don't let it go to your head. Izzy's leash is hanging in the bedroom closet."

She watched Gavin and Izzy cross the large suite to the door for the adjoining bedroom. When he opened the door, Piper could see that the overhead light was on. Still, she hoped Sofia would be resting. The teenager had been placated when Gavin had given her the computer tablet with the live-feed of her father in the hospital. All in all, Sofia had handled the threat and inherent danger with a great deal more composure than Piper had shown.

Winston called upon her to concentrate on the computer sketch. Together, they studied each feature. At her instruction, he made tweaks to the shape of the ears and the jawline. When she looked away and quickly looked back, she noticed slight adjustments until, finally, after twenty-five minutes, she considered the picture to be accurate.

"That's him," she said. "He's the shooter."

The door to the suite swung open for Gavin and Izzy. A light mist glistened on the shoulders of his jacket, and droplets sparkled in his wavy brown hair. When Izzy wove her way through the several detectives and marshals in the room to end up at Piper's side, she smelled like wet dog and her fur was damp.

Marshal Johnson came into the suite from the adjoining room with Sofia in tow. Predictably, she was complaining. "It's almost three. About time for you guys to get your act together."

The lead police detective apologized and explained that he needed her information as soon as possible so their investigation could get underway.

Sofia slouched into a chair at the table. "I don't know what I can tell you. I wasn't at the house when that creep shot my dad."

The detective cleared his throat. "How often have you visited the Offenbach Community Farm Project?"

"The commune has nothing to do with the shooting."

"Your boyfriend is Logan Offenbach, correct?"

Her eyebrows pulled down in a scowl. "We haven't defined our relationship. I'm not sure 'boyfriend' is the term I'd use."

"Have you introduced Logan to your father? Does Marco approve of the young man?"

Piper cringed. The aggressive questioning tactics were more likely to irritate Sofia than to elicit any information.

"What are you saying?" Sofia bolted to her feet. "Logan isn't a suspect. He was with me. I'm his—what's it called? His alibi, I'm his alibi. And I'm totally reliable. You can ask McQueen."

All eyes turned to Gavin. He studied a computer printout of Winston's finished sketch in his hand, then stalked across the suite to a stack of folders on the table. He plucked out an eight-by-ten photograph and held it beside the computer sketch. "Looks like a match to me."

The detective squinted at the photo and the sketch. "Right down to the missing tooth. What's the young man's name?"

"Taimar Drako," Gavin said.

Sofia rose slowly from the chair by the table. Staring at the photograph, she paced across the room and back again. "I've seen this guy before. He's been hanging out at the commune with Dmitri and his friends."

"That's where our investigation will start." The

detective straightened his shoulders. "Tell me, Sofia, do your farming friends get up and get busy at sunrise?"

"Not fair." Her voice quivered. "What are you going to do to Logan? To the other people who live there?"

"If they haven't broken any laws, no problem. We're only interested in the person who shot your father."

Taimar Drako. A clear, new focus to the investigation had to be a good thing, right? Piper wasn't so sure.

THIN SHARDS OF morning sunlight pierced the thick cloud cover. Though it was after 10:00 a.m., the cars had their headlights on as they slashed through the light but steady rain. Taimar Drako adjusted his waterproof camo poncho and ducked low behind thick shrubs on the forested hillside opposite the "Pets Welcome" hotel. Not taking any chances, he'd parked his bike up the hill on a remote trail and climbed down to this surveillance position across the road, approximately three hundred yards from the hotel entrance. If he'd been armed with an AK-47 or a sniper rifle, the guests coming and going on the sidewalk would be in range. But Tai only had the laughable .25-caliber, lousy for accuracy at a distance. If he fired the sissy little handgun, he'd only draw attention to himself.

Not that he was supposed to use a weapon of any sort. His instructions from his father and from Tom

Ivanov himself barred him from engaging with the police. Only observe. Like a pathetic, weak-kneed punk, he was supposed to stand by and watch. Tai aimed his long-range binoculars at the fourth-floor rooms where the curtains were still drawn.

Last night, Tai had received the tip that had led him to this Beaverton hotel not too far from Nike headquarters. Then he'd dismissed his helpers from the Offenbach commune and promised to contact them again, which he never would. Dmitri and his ilk were expendable—wannabe criminals excited by the prospect of being part of the legendary Dragons.

After a sweeping scan with the binoculars, Tai watched another unmarked car pull away from the drive leading to the hotel door. There had been dozens of them, coming and going. The cops were up to something, and he wanted to know their plans. All this waiting was getting on his nerves. He needed action.

He dug into a pocket. Only one energy bar left. Then he'd be out of food, and he didn't dare to step away and refuel. If he lost track of the witnesses, his father would be furious. Ivanov would probably shoot him.

And then…he saw the dog, an ugly mutt prancing along the sidewalk at the end of a bright red leash. Though prohibited from shooting, Tai drew his handgun and pointed the barrel at the damn dog. Killing the animal wasn't as important as shooting its owner, the witness to Tai's assault on Marco. She could cause him trouble. He shifted his aim toward her. She talked and laughed with that federal marshal, another person he'd like to shoot but wouldn't. Just the woman. And that damn bitch of a dog.

Chapter Ten

In deference to the rainy morning, Gavin had changed from black leather to a waterproof gray jacket from the go-bag he always kept in the back of his SUV. A Seattle Mariners baseball cap covered his head. From one of the female detectives, he'd arranged to borrow a clean shirt and a bright blue rain jacket for Piper. She'd pulled the hood up when they'd moved away from the covered hotel entrance.

Though three plainclothes officers acted as body-guards and the surrounding area had been searched, Gavin didn't feel completely secure. Taking Piper and Izzy for a walk held a certain amount of risk, but he needed to grab a few minutes alone with her, partly to reassure her and partly because he appreci-ated how helpful she'd been in creating the sketch of Taimar Drako. Gavin wanted Piper to be on his side instead of building barriers every time he got close.

His right hand rested on the butt of his Beretta, ready to pull the gun in case of threat. He main-tained a brisk pace along the sidewalk. His plan: go out, clear the air between them, and move on to the next order of business. Simple.

He glanced over at her. "Do you want an umbrella?"

"I don't mind the rain." When she tilted her face toward his, droplets spattered her rosy cheeks and caught in her thick, dark eyelashes. Her blue eyes shimmered.

"After lunch, we're going to see Marco at the hospital."

"I thought you said a hospital visit was dangerous." She jogged a few steps to keep up with his longer strides. "Somebody could ambush us."

"You're right. I said that. And I meant it. The threat is still there, and I don't want you to forget that. Not for one minute. Danger is everywhere."

"Are you being a tiny bit overdramatic?"

He gestured toward the rushing waters of Johnston Creek behind the hotel. "An assassin could be hiding down there in the weeds and bog plants." He pointed in the opposite direction across the four-lane divided road. "A sniper might take a position on that far hillside with the pines and larches."

She followed his gaze and shuddered. "Point taken."

"But I don't think anybody knows we're staying here. Plus, we've had outstanding cooperation and protection from local law enforcement. And we're taking precautions. You're wearing your bulletproof vest, right?"

"Right." She thumped the Kevlar with her free

hand. "And I appreciate the effort. Ever since Winston finished that sketch, I can't stop thinking about Taimar Drako."

Taimar, the grandson, didn't worry Gavin nearly as much as Ivanov, the escaped convict who was headed to the West Coast. According to Marshal Esposito, Ivanov had been seen at an airfield in Colorado where he'd tried to steal a Cessna Citation. FBI computer chatter from reliable sources had hinted at the possibility of a terrorist action using an airplane. With Ivanov in play, that scenario became more likely. The pilot's skill with a wide variety of aircraft was well-deserved. And he'd grown up in the United States, speaking English without an accent and looking like a friendly, middle-aged guy with brown hair and brown eyes. No tats. No scars. No distinguishing features.

Gavin gestured to a sidewalk that skirted the edge of a vacant lot beside the hotel. "We'll circle that area and get back to the rooms."

"Thanks for bringing me outside," she said. "I love Sofia dearly and she has a lovely voice, but I need my quiet time. I miss my cabin."

Her voice held a note of longing and he wished he could satisfy her needs. "I'd like to visit your little hideaway."

"It's quiet and pristine. On rainy days like this, the mist twines through the moss-covered trees, making everything mysterious. And when the sun shines, the Yamhill forest is an incredible little ecosystem, endlessly fascinating."

"Not like corporate life in Atlanta?"

"That's an ecosystem all its own. With a food chain and predators and prey. Survival of the most ambitious." She stopped while Izzy moved off the sidewalk into the wild grass and stuck her nose into a golden dogwood shrub. "When can I go home?"

"I'm not sure." He stopped beside her and looked over her head at the forested hillside across the road. "I'm going to level with you, Piper. I appreciate your insights, and I think you can assist the investigation. We can work together, you and me."

"How do I know I can trust you?"

"You don't." He shrugged.

"Okay. I'm listening."

"I suspect that Sofia told you about the Dragons, the *troika* and Marco's Russian roots."

"How do you know that?"

"When I mentioned Sofia's mother, I saw your empathy. You know the story of that tragedy. And you fidget when I talk about Drako. Also—just now— you admitted that my assumption was correct."

Piper stuck out her chin. "I'm sure Sofia didn't say anything she wasn't supposed to."

Because this teenager never rebelled against the rules? "I respect you for keeping her secret, but you've got to realize that it's not altogether accurate. Sofia gave you recollections from when she was ten years old. You need to hear the grown-up version."

"I thought this was supposed to be hush-hush."

"You're already up to your knees in supposedly

secret information, might as well take the plunge. Are you ready to help? You and Izzy?"

"Yes."

Not standard procedure, but she already knew more than half of the story and was a witness to a related assault. Izzy finished her sniffing, and Gavin stepped up the pace. "Yuri Drako—an immigrant in his nineties—ran several domestic terrorist groups called the Dragons. His primary group, the *troika*, operated out of Jersey. They planned to hijack a plane from Liberty International Airport in Newark then use the passengers in a hostage exchange to free several of their comrades in prison."

"Marco's testimony stopped them," she said. "Standing up to the Dragons was a brave thing to do."

"Heroic," he agreed. "Thanks to Marco, the FBI shut down the hijacking, scooped up hundreds of illegal weapons and enough explosives to level the entire Newark terminal. Hundreds could have been killed. The feds also derailed other plots in other parts of the country. Drako, Ivanov and two less important members of the Dragons were tried, convicted and sentenced to many years in federal prisons."

"Do the Dragons still exist?"

"They remain an ongoing threat, mostly involved in white-collar crimes like money laundering and extortion. They're extremely well financed." They paused while Izzy did her business. "During the hijacking scheme, the pilot of the plane they planned to commandeer was murdered in cold blood. And we lost a rookie marshal. Her name was Dawn Wain-wright, and she was twenty-eight. Her name is on the Honor Roll at USMS headquarters in Arlington."

"I'm so sorry to hear of her death." Piper cleaned up after Izzy and they headed back toward the hotel entrance. "It sounds like the Dragons have their fingers in a lot of different pies. Why won't they leave Marco and Sofia alone?"

"Remember that old proverb. Revenge is a dish best served cold."

"I've heard it."

"For six years, Ivanov, Drako and two others have been in federal penitentiaries. I doubt that a single day passed when they didn't curse Marco Barbieri, aka Maxim Lombardi, and his daughter. They've had a long time to plan."

"Oh my God." She stamped along the sidewalk, splashing through puddles. "When I think of those monsters watching Sofia sing 'Let it Go' on social media and plotting ways to harm her, it makes me sick. Is Drako still running the show?"

"Yuri Drako is ninety-six years old and terminally ill. His very expensive team of lawyers managed to get him a compassionate transfer to the penitentiary in Sheridan."

"That's less than an hour from where I live," she said.

"His only family—a son and grandson—have a house on the coast and visit him in jail from time to time. From what I hear, the old man has a private room with all the medical equipment he needs and a team of hot nurses."

"But he's a prisoner."

"Drako pays their salaries."

Her lip curled in disgust. "Are you going to interrogate him?"

"Not my assignment." Gavin's responsibility was keeping his WITSEC people—Marco and Sofia—safe. And watching out for Piper, who seemed a likely candidate for protective custody. "DJ is investigating the shooting. This morning, he went to the Offenbach commune with local police. They arrested Dmitri and his buddies when they identified Tai from the mug shot."

"But they didn't know where to find Tai Drako?"

When she looked to him for a response, her forehead tensed and her lips flattened. The fear and anger she'd held at bay had almost caught up with her. He wished he could offer comfort, but the danger was too real. "Tai might be headed to his father's home near Devil's Lake. Sorry I don't have better news."

With her free hand, she brushed a strand of dark auburn hair off her forehead. "I appreciate hearing the truth. These Dragons aren't just petty criminals, and their medieval devotion to cold revenge is horrific. Now I understand why you hover over us."

He wanted to tell her that everything would be all right. The bad guys would be locked up, and the good guys would be able to return to their normal lives. It might happen. But probably not. Slowly, he exhaled and offered a final bit of information. "DJ will speak to Yuri Drako in prison, either through a computer hookup or in person, probably this afternoon."

Under her breath, she muttered, "I have a few choice comments I'd like to make to that old dragon."

"But you won't. You've got to keep everything we've talked about to yourself, Piper. You don't have to lie, but we're not going to do group discussions of the crimes. And whatever you do…" He paused for emphasis. "Don't tell Sofia."

About fifty yards from the front entrance, Izzy came to a screeching halt. She arched her back and stuck her sensitive nose into the air. She sniffed to the left and then to the right, then twirled in a circle. Facing the forested hillside on the other side of the divided road, Izzy lowered her front paws and stuck her tail in the air. She'd made a sighting.

"What is it?" Piper asked. "Something on that hill?"

"No way," he said. "She can't smell across four lanes of traffic. That's got to be three or four hundred yards away."

Piper moved closer to the dog and asked again. "Izzy, what is it?"

When the mutt gave a low growl, Gavin had the distinct impression that Izzy didn't like what she'd located. He stared through the rain into the thickets of trees and shrubs. At the moment he thought he spotted a black, metal cylinder, he heard a harsh pop, like the noise a car makes when it backfires. But he knew the bang hadn't come from a car.

He heard a second gunshot. And a third.

He reached for Piper, but she slipped away from him and dove to the sidewalk. Her arms wrapped around Izzy, pulling her down. Piper protected the dog with her own body.

Gavin motioned to the plainclothes police who were acting as bodyguards. "Over here," he directed. "Take her and the dog inside."

Using his two-way radio communication, he alerted the other officers in the area that they had an active shooter on the hillside opposite the hotel. As soon as he ducked into the lobby, Piper threw her arms around his neck. Her hood fell back and her long hair spilled over her shoulders. He held her tightly. This was his fault. He'd taken a risk and was damn lucky his carelessness hadn't resulted in disaster.

Izzy had done a better job of protecting. Reaching down to pat her forehead, Gavin marveled at the dog's ability to scent danger from such a distance. Had the shooter been aiming at them or at Izzy?

IN THE HOTEL BEDROOM, Piper stood at the window with the drapes still closed and tried to peek around the edge of the window frame. Several officers were searching the forested hillside across the road, but she could barely see them. Continuing rain limited her visibility, and the autumn foliage got in the way. If Gavin hadn't poked his head into the room a few minutes ago and informed them that spent shell casings for a .22-caliber pistol had been found, she might have dismissed the whole incident as something she'd imagined. And she would have been wrong. The shell casings were proof. Someone had fired shots at her and Izzy.

Sofia sat yoga-style in the middle of her bed, staring obsessively at the blank computer tablet that had shown Marco in his hospital bed. The nurses had requested that she turn off the feed while they took her father for tests, but he'd been awake and able to talk for a few minutes.

"He told me the pain wasn't too bad." Her tone of voice was soft and miserable. "He made a joke about losing weight and needing pasta."

Piper went to her own bed, nearly tripping over Izzy. Since the shooting incident, the dog had been glued to her side. "We'll be able to see your dad in person soon."

"Do you think I should tell him about me and Logan?"

"Might be best if he concentrates on getting better." Piper had a whole new respect for Marco's bravery and the risk he'd taken when he'd stood up to the Dragons. He was a good man who'd tried to do the right thing, but Piper couldn't predict how a protective father would react to his daughter's dating relationship. "I'm not sure what you're going to say. When you mentioned Logan before, you didn't even want to call him your boyfriend."

"Then all this stuff happened." Sofia slid her slender body off the bed to the floor and cuddled Izzy. "We might have to move to another city, and I don't want to break things off with Logan."

"I'm sure Marshal McQueen can work something out."

"Ha!" Sofia tossed her head. This morning, she'd parted her hair in the middle and made two long braids. "After getting shot at, he's going to be super protective. Make us wear suits of armor or layers of bubble wrapping. I'm totally amazed that he's still okay with a hospital visit."

After her truthful talk with Gavin, Piper had a different opinion of the man. Yes, he was intensely protective. But that was his job. And he had good reason to be wary of the Dragons and their devotion to cold revenge.

Still, she knew better than to waste her breath trying to change Sofia's mind. In spite of the braids and the purple eyeshadow that matched her long ombré sweatshirt, this young lady was neither flighty nor silly. She knew what she wanted and didn't hesitate to go after it.

"Tell me about Logan. How did you meet?"

A sweet smile curved Sofia's lips. Eyelashes fluttered, and her green eyes went dreamy when she talked about her tall, lean, handsome, blond boyfriend. Her experiences with him sounded like typical examples of girl-meets-boy. If Piper hadn't witnessed their passionate kiss when they'd fled from the Offenbach commune, she wouldn't have thought there was much of a physical relationship. Probing for more information on that topic, she asked, "Is he a good kisser?"

"I don't have much experience, but yeah. He's really gentle, and when he glides his tongue into my mouth, it makes me…" She shivered. "You know what I'm talking about. You were married."

Memories of her disaster of a marriage bore no resemblance to Sofia's romantic ideals. "Nothing better than a good kiss, it's almost as good as…the other stuff."

"Is Marshal McQueen a good kisser?"

"What?" Her jaw dropped and she gaped. "Why would you ask that?"

"I've seen how he looks at you. If you haven't already kissed, it's coming, and I think it's coming real soon."

"You're wrong."

Before they could delve more deeply, Gavin knocked at the door and stepped inside. "The investigators found tire tracks for a small motorcycle, a match for those we found outside Marco's house. Same guy. Same shooter."

Piper averted her gaze, avoiding direct confrontation with this good-looking man who'd broken all the rules to tell her the truth. *Do I want him to kiss me?* "He got away."

"Not surprising. It took the police several minutes to get across the road, especially since they were pursuing an armed suspect and needed to use caution." He paused. "The real question is, why he did he bother to fire a .22-caliber handgun from that distance? Either he knows nothing about guns or he just wasn't thinking straight."

"Actually, the real question," she said quietly, "is how did he know where we were staying?"

"I don't see how it's possible, but he must have followed us."

"On his little motorcycle? Wouldn't we have noticed?"

"Oh, wait. I've got an idea," Sofia said eagerly as she climbed off the floor onto the bed. "Dmitri and the guys from the commune could have used a bunch of cars and trucks to track us."

"Doubtful," Gavin said. "They've already been arrested and said nothing."

"Arrested." She frowned. "Logan will hate that."

"How do you know what Logan thinks?"

Suspicion wove through Gavin's voice, and Piper felt the same way. She and Sofia had surrendered their phones, the hotel landline had been removed, and the tablet with Marco's face only had that one channel.

Sofia shook her shoulders. "Omigod, you guys. I'm just guessing. Logan lives at the commune. Of course, he'd hate arrests in his own backyard."

"We'll talk about this later," Gavin said. "For now, you need to pack up your things and get ready to go. When we leave for the hospital, we won't be coming back to this hotel."

Sofia groaned. "But I like this place."

"Our location has been compromised," he said. "Obviously."

Piper dared to glance up at his face. His jaw was

set. His deep-set brown eyes glistened with hidden meaning, and his lips formed a silent word. *Sorry.*

She nodded forgiveness.

Sofia flopped backward on the bed and groaned. "Omigod, you two. If we weren't already in a hotel, I'd tell you to get a room."

Chapter Eleven

When they arrived at the hospital, Piper couldn't believe the extreme security precautions. Their convoy of three black SUVs halted at the covered entrance. Four heavily armed bodyguards from Portland SWAT emerged to form a cordon around her, Sofia and Izzy. In tight formation, they marched through the front doors, and Piper wished she could shrink to the size of an acorn and bounce through the halls unnoticed. She didn't like excessive attention. This sort of scene was more appropriate for royalty and/or Third World dictators.

Walking beside her, Gavin complimented himself. "Not bad. With these SWAT bodyguards, I doubt any of the psycho-Dragons will dare come near us."

"I hate it," she muttered.

"Izzy seems pleased."

With a wildly wagging tail, the mutt danced through the hospital corridors with head held high. She accepted compliments and head pats from nurses in scrubs, patients and lab techs in white coats. Sofia wasn't much better. She waved to her supposedly adoring public and flashed wide smiles. Once, she paused for a selfie with a little girl in a wheelchair.

Head down, Piper boarded an elevator with Gavin, and he made sure the two of them were alone. "Hey," she said, "isn't it dangerous to separate from Sofia?"

"She has three bodyguards and Izzy." As soon as the doors snapped shut, he gathered her into an embrace. His lips were close to hers, but they weren't kissing. "I needed this moment with you."

"Worth the risk?" she asked.

"Yes."

Being pressed against his solid, muscular chest felt so warm and wonderful that she swallowed her other objections. "Sofia seems to be handling this just fine."

"Fine," he echoed.

"Even though she's desperately worried about her dad, she's a natural when it comes to adoring crowds. Someday, she'll be a fabulous celebrity."

"Someday."

When he released her, his arm brushed the side of her breast, sending a distracting tremor straight to her core. Catching her breath, she asked, "Is there anything I should say to Marco? Anything you need to find out?"

"Before he was shot, I sensed that he had information he hadn't shared with me. Matter of fact, that was one of the reasons I was headed to his house."

"You think he's keeping a secret?" *Weren't they all?*

Gavin shrugged. "If he's decided to drop out of

the WITSEC program, that's his choice. But I want to be informed of his plans."

The elevator doors opened on the fifth floor and they stepped out to await the arrival of Sofia and Izzy. Piper guessed that Marco's room was at the end of the hall where two more guards were posted, and she was glad that he'd been quickly released from ICU. In that restricted area, Izzy wouldn't have been a welcome visitor. Since the mutt had accompanied Piper on visits to her uncle after his heart attack, Izzy was familiar with hospital protocol. The dog knew she was supposed to be quiet and not get in the way, but there were so many diversions. Not only the unusual beeping noises and antiseptic smells, but hospitals were filled with nice people who wanted Izzy's attention. The dog was a more social animal than Piper.

As soon as Sofia emerged from the elevator, she charged down the hall to where the guards were standing. Both Piper and Gavin had expected this response. Neither tried to get in her way when she burst into her father's room. They followed quickly behind her.

At the foot of his bed, she halted and stared at Marco Barbieri, who was usually boisterous and full of life. The gunshot wounds had taken a toll. Though sitting up against the pillows, his large body seemed deflated. The glaring white bandages on his shoulder wound contrasted his dull skin. His eyes were closed. He had an oxygen cannula in his nose and

IV fluids dripping into his arm while beeping machines monitored his blood pressure and heartbeat.

Sofia held her hand over her mouth to stifle a gasp, but she couldn't stop tears from streaking down her cheeks. A nurse in purple scrubs—roughly the same color as Sofia's eye shadow—pointed her to a chair beside his bed and placed a tissue in her trembling hand.

"You can talk to him," the nurse encouraged.

"Papa? Oh, Papa, I'm sorry. So sorry."

On the other side of the bed, Izzy stood quietly. Piper joined Sofia and rested her hand on the young woman's shoulder. Together, they watched as Marco opened his eyes. "Sofia," he whispered, *"ti amo tanto."*

"And I love you, Papa." Her voice choked into silence. "So much, I love you so much."

Marco's gaze lifted and he looked directly at Piper. "My friend, do you have the truffles?"

"They're in the car."

"I told her to bring them," Sofia said. "If we'd left them at the house, they'd be part of a crime scene, and you'd never be able to use them."

"Attenzione, Piper. Listen to me. Take the truffles to Bella Trattoria and give them to Rosa for the sanctuary." Using his arms for leverage, he forced himself to lean forward. Two of the machines monitoring his condition squawked in protest. "Only to Chef Rosa. For the sanctuary."

"Whatever you say." Reaching around Sofia, she took his arm and guided him back to a more comfortable-looking position. She repeated the name of the Beaverton restaurant where he worked part-time and the name of the chef. "Should I mention the sanctuary?"

"Yes." With surprising vigor, he waved to Gavin, who stood by the door. "Hey, McQueen, make sure she delivers the truffles. You will do this for me?"

"Absolutely." Under his breath, he mumbled so quietly that few but Piper could hear. "I don't get it. The man has been shot and targeted by violent domestic terrorists, and he's worried about mush-rooms."

Piper scowled at him then turned back toward her old friend. The last time she'd seen Marco, he'd been bloody and unconscious. She didn't know the scope of the medical procedures he'd undergone, but his recovery time was impressive. "You seem to be doing well."

"Takes more than a popgun to put me down." His bravado was strong, but his energy faded. He leaned back against the pillows and closed his eyes. "I feel better now. I needed to make sure my girl was taken care of. My beautiful Sofia."

"Moof," Izzy said.

Marco attempted to laugh but coughed instead. "Izzy, you're beautiful, too."

The nurse stepped up beside them. Gently, she placed Sofia's slender fingers atop her father's wrist. "He's doing remarkably well, but he still needs rest. Sorry, but I've got to limit your visiting time. Run along and check back with me in an hour."

Gavin came forward. "I need the answer to one question."

"Make it quick."

He approached on the side of the bed where Izzy had positioned herself. "Marco, you mentioned to Piper that we should look for the grandson. Were you talking about Yuri Drako's grandson?"

"Yes."

"How did you know Drako had a grandson?"

"We spoke on the computer."

Gavin reacted as though he'd been punched in the nose. "Tell me again. Who did you speak to?"

"Yuri Drako."

A flush of anger darkened Gavin's expression. His dark eyes flared like embers. "Have you spoken to him more than once? When was the last time?"

"He's sick. Tired." Marco's voice lowered to a husky whisper. "Yuri is too old for crime. Doesn't wish me harm."

"Why did he send his grandson to your doorstep with a gun?"

Marco slowly rolled his head from side to side, and the nurse stepped in. "I'm sorry, Marshal, but I must end your questioning. It's time for all of you to go. Now."

Sofia kissed her father's cheek. "Please don't make me leave. I'll sit here and be quiet. Won't say a word."

"She'll sing for me," Marco whispered. "Softly."

Sofia looked up at the nurse, pleading with her big, green eyes. "Please."

"Quietly," the nurse said. "The rest of you and the dog, come with me."

Before they left the room, Piper glanced over her shoulder. She saw Sofia gently stroking her father's hand and heard her murmuring the words to "Greensleeves." The sweet bond between father and daughter touched her heart.

DRIVEN BY BARELY controlled anger, Gavin stormed the length of the fifth-floor corridor, past the central nurses' station to a waiting area at the far end. He stood and stared through a window at patchy clouds in a steel-gray sky. His pulse hammered in his ears. His chest constricted. Breathing hard, he couldn't fill his lungs. Not enough air. The hospital wasn't big enough to contain his rage. The light green walls of the corridor closed in. Too tight. Suffocating. He had to get out of there. What the hell had Marco been thinking? Why did he agree to talk with Yuri Drako? To allow that dragon to poison his mind?

The contact between them went against everything WITSEC stood for. The purpose of the program was to keep Marco separate from his enemies. The old man had blatantly flouted the rules.

Had Drako contacted Marco or the other way around? How long had this been going on? Did they ever meet in person? Question piled upon question, and Gavin felt certain he wouldn't like the answers. He stalked back to where Piper and Izzy were standing. After he spoke to the guards outside Marco's room and told them not to allow Sofia to leave, he approached Piper.

"Let's go." He signaled for her and Izzy to follow. "Take the stairs. I need the exercise."

She joined him in the stairwell, and he appreciated that she didn't feel compelled to make a comment or ask where they were going. As she descended, Piper maintained a cool, nonjudgmental attitude. Izzy bounded down the stairs and back up and down again. When she gave a full-throated bark, the sound echoed against the concrete walls.

On the first floor, he directed Piper and Izzy to a side exit where the three black SUVs were waiting. The rain had dissipated to a drizzle, but the late-afternoon skies were still overcast. Gavin commandeered the first vehicle in line, held the door for Piper and Izzy, then went around to the other side to get behind the steering wheel. The engine started with a reassuring growl, and he merged onto the street. "Okay, Piper, how do I get to Bella Trattoria?"

"Haven't you been there before?"

"A couple of times with Marco."

"Use the GPS in the car." While he programmed the location, she twisted around in her seat to search in the back seat. "Aha, lucky for us the truffles are in this SUV. If they hadn't been here, we'd have to go back and search the other two cars."

He didn't understand these people, including Piper, and their concern about these weird, fancy mushrooms. *What was the big deal?* Marco worried more about truffles than contact from a violent terrorist currently incarcerated in a federal penitentiary. "Why did Marco talk to Drako? He had to be aware of the Dragon's vows of revenge."

"Shocked me, too," she admitted. "The most important person in Marco's world is his daughter. Talking to Drako puts her in danger."

Her voice struck the right chord with him, and he was glad she realized that Marco had made a potentially fatal mistake that they needed to correct. When he glanced over at her in the passenger seat, he saw empathy and concern in her crystal-blue eyes. "Thanks for coming with me."

"I'm amazed you're willing to drop off the truffles with Chef Rosa."

"I promised."

"Marco made sure he got your agreement, didn't he?"

"And I needed space." If he hadn't left the hospital, his rising frustration might have erupted like Mount St. Helens in 1980. "This trip to the trattoria is a good excuse to get away, and I'll be glad to have the damn truffles taken care of."

"It's not their fault." A light grin teased the corners of her mouth, and he noticed that when she smiled her chin sharpened. Her face became even more heart-shaped. "From what I hear, Marco gave Chef Rosa his prized recipe for beef stroganoff with two different kinds of mushrooms and black truffles grated over the noodles."

"Can't wait to try it," he said sarcastically.

"Have you ever eaten any of his food?"

"Oh, yeah. To know Marco is to be fed by him. Spaghetti carbonara, cioppino, and pizza, lots of pizza. He's a talented chef."

"And he sacrificed his restaurant to protect his daughter. It makes no sense for him to be friendly with Drako. He knows the risk."

Gavin had seen this sort of reversal in other witnesses. After spending years away from former friends and associates, they craved well-remembered sights and the sound of a familiar voice, even when the person speaking was an enemy. It didn't do any good to complain about Marco's bad judgment. Gavin had to accept what happened. *Spilt milk.*

"Moving on," he said. "As soon as Marco is stronger, he needs to tell us everything Drako said. Maybe the old Dragon explained why Ivanov is racing across the country." Gavin hoped Drako had outsmarted himself. "He might have betrayed their plans."

With Piper's help, he followed the GPS instructions through Beaverton toward the area where Marco and Sofia lived. Their timing coincided with rush hour, but traffic wasn't bad. In less than twenty minutes, he parked the SUV at the kitchen entrance to Bella Trattoria, a well-landscaped stone-and-stucco building with red, white and green awnings and a tiled roof.

Leaving Izzy in the vehicle with a window cracked, Piper took her insulated carrier with the truffles, went to the door and entered without knocking. Gavin followed.

Though it was only a few hours past four o'clock,

the huge kitchen bustled with men and women in chef's coats and aprons. All seemed intent on their tasks—chopping, stirring, mixing or tasting. Gavin had visited with Marco two or three times before and had been amazed at the way such delicious food emerged from the kitchen chaos.

Piper dodged between stainless-steel tables toward a bubbling cauldron on a stovetop where a short, round woman wearing a long pinstriped apron stirred with a wooden spoon. "Chef Rosa, I brought you some truffles from Marco Barbieri."

When the woman looked up from the cauldron, it was obvious she'd been weeping. Her brown eyes were red-rimmed. "*Ciao*, Piper. Tell me, please tell me, that Marco is okay."

"The doctors say he'll make a full recovery."

The two women embraced and held each other, giving solace and exchanging their fears for Marco. Though Piper considered herself to be a hermit of sorts, Gavin suspected she had many friends who were as affectionate as Chef Rosa. When she whispered the word "sanctuary," Rosa led them both to a small, cluttered office at the back of the kitchen.

After she closed the door, Rosa looked up at Gavin. "I know you, Marshal McQueen. How could you let this happen to Marco?"

"Sanctuary," he said. "What does it mean?"

"About a year ago, Marco told me that if he ever got in trouble and couldn't take care of Sofia, I was to deliver this message to her." She dug into a middle desk drawer and removed a sealed white envelope. "I didn't open it, but I can feel the outline of a house key."

Written in black ink across the back was a single word. *Sanctuary.* Gavin knew what it meant. Marco had arranged a safe place for his daughter to stay.

Chapter Twelve

In the Pacific Northwest, coffee was more than a beverage. It was a lifestyle—one that Piper had happily embraced when she'd moved to Oregon. At her cabin, she followed a morning ritual of grinding the beans, measuring selected free-trade coffee and taking the first delicious taste while it was so hot that the liquid almost burned her tongue. After dinner, she sipped a decaf latte. And when she was in Portland, she took every opportunity to treat herself.

The cafeteria at Overton Hospital offered fresh-brewed varieties in dark roast, blond, chicory and decaf as well as espresso drinks prepared by a barista. Piper ordered a double-shot, almond-milk latte and carried her cup to the table where Gavin had laid out a couple of plates and silverware from the cafeteria line. He opened her insulated bag. The truffles—all except three small ones she'd saved for training—had been left at Bella Trattoria as Marco had instructed. In exchange, Chef Rosa had packed food for their dinner. He opened the bag.

The aroma of Italian spices masked the antiseptic

hospital smell and the bland scent of cafeteria food. Gavin slipped off his jacket, rolled up his shirtsleeves and adjusted the black fleece vest that was just long enough to hide the Beretta holstered on his belt. He placed a fire-roasted calzone wrapped in foil in front of her and set another on his plate.

Izzy exhaled a doggy sigh, obviously feeling left out.

"Sorry, girl," Gavin said, "no calzone for you."

When he cut into the sausage, mozzarella, tomato and Hatch chili turnover, and forked a bite into his mouth, he moaned with pleasure. His eyes closed as he savored. "Amazing."

His immense satisfaction amused her. "Almost better than sex, right?"

His eyes popped open. "Not a fair comparison."

"Why not?" She sipped her latte.

"Good sex requires the right atmosphere, soft music, visual stimulation and, obviously, the right partner. I'd enjoy this calzone if I was eating it blindfolded in an ice bath surrounded by alligators and listening to car horns." He cut off another bite. "Chef Rosa wanted me to give one of these to Marco. That's not going to happen."

"Are you punishing him for talking to Yuri?"

"Not really. I'm just being selfish." He shrugged. "It's been a rough day."

She agreed. From the mysterious shooter this morning to Marco's reported conversation with the Dragon to Chef Rosa handing over a key and directions to a sanctuary in the Coastal Range near Tillamook, Gavin had been hit by one problem after another. The most recent complication had come when they'd returned to the hospital room and caught one of his doctors on his late-afternoon rounds. Though Marco's overall prognosis was good, the doc recommended that the patient stay in the hospital for two or three more days so they could monitor his condition, watch for infection and possible sepsis. In a final twist of annoying setbacks, Sofia had demanded that Gavin arrange a meeting between Logan and her father. Never mind his position as a marshal meant limiting contact with outsiders. Or considering her father's health. Gavin had turned her down and she'd been furious.

Piper skipped the calzone, reached into the insulated bag and found a creamy, delicious cannoli pastry that made a better complement for her latte. "Where do we go from here?"

"I have two possibilities for where we can stay tonight. A motel that isn't as nice as the 'Pets Welcome' place. No 24/7 room service. No swimming pool. No special treats for Izzy. But it's clean. Or an FBI safe house outside Portland."

"Or Marco's sanctuary," she added. "Even if you don't approve, you've got to consider the possibility. It might be perfect."

He chewed while he considered. "From a protection standpoint, the hotel and the FBI safe house are better alternatives. If we're attacked, I can call for immediate backup."

"Can you trust them?" She licked a bit of the sweet

mascarpone filling from the cannoli. "Didn't you say that you suspected a leak? The only way the shooter could have known where we were staying was if somebody on the inside tipped him off."

"It bothers me that we might have a rat." Apparently, his worries didn't interfere with his eating. He finished off the calzone before continuing. "There were all kinds of cops, feds and marshals rolling in and out of the hotel last night and this morning. I had no time to vet them all. One or more of them could be on the Dragon's payroll."

"If we go to the sanctuary, nobody will know where we are."

"There's a certain appeal to that," he said. "But I don't trust Marco's judgment. His idea of a sanctuary might include a scenic view of the coast, a hot tub and a fantastic kitchen. What we really need is top-notch security."

"I'm pretty sure we'll have solitude. Population is sparse in that area. Very few people but lots of wildlife. The spruce and hemlock forests are abundant and unspoiled. Izzy and I can practice truffle hunting."

"We're not going on vacation." He placed a foil-wrapped calzone to his right and a cannoli to his left. "I've got a big decision here. Sweet or spicy."

"Why not both?"

"Smart lady, that's why I like you."

She knew he was joking but still felt a little thrill. *He likes me.* Taking a big bite from her cannoli, she leaned over her plate so she wouldn't get powdered sugar all down the front of her navy blue T-shirt. "Mmm, this is super good."

He took a sip from his water glass and unwrapped the calzone. "Maybe we should stay at the FBI house tonight and explore Marco's sanctuary tomorrow."

Not her decision, and she was awfully glad she didn't need to take on that responsibility. When she'd worked in the corporate world, Piper had run into plenty of traitors, turncoats and spies, but the stakes had never been this high. A business betrayal might mean losing an account or running over budget. If a double agent sold them out to the Dragons and botched their protection, they might pay with their lives.

Halfway through the second calzone, Gavin abandoned the knife and fork to hold the spicy meat pie in his hand. Every other bite, he paused to lick his fingers. There was something reassuring about watching a healthy man enjoy his food. It was simple. Natural. Normal. Piper felt no need to comment.

He waved toward the cafeteria entrance when DJ entered the dining room. The tall, blond marshal flexed his shoulders, waved back and sauntered toward them. Though she knew that he and Gavin hadn't coordinated their outfits, they wore nearly identical clothes: khaki trousers, button-down shirt, thermal vest and a holstered sidearm. DJ topped off his look with a beige cowboy hat that he removed when he sat at their table and nodded to her. He focused on Gavin, more specifically, on the remains of Gavin's calzone.

"Did you leave a taste for me?" DJ asked as he reached down to pat Izzy on the head.

"Not sure you deserve one of these," Gavin said. "What did you find out about Taimar?"

"After a visit to the commune this morning, I went to his father's house in Devil's Lake. The guy has taste. Parked out front is a forest-green Hummer EV, an electric car with style and power. And his house is classy with high ceilings, open beams and tall windows. It's the kind of floor plan me and Chelsey are looking for."

Gavin shot her a glance. "DJ's brain isn't totally in the game. All he can talk about is his new wife. He got married a couple of months ago."

"Three months and four days," he said with a ridiculously wide grin.

Piper noticed a blush staining his cheeks. "Congratulations."

"Thanks," he said. "There's one thing about the house that Chelsey would hate. Josef Drako has a bunch of animal heads hanging on the walls. Hunting trophies, he calls them. Wolverine, elk, black bear, mountain lion and such."

Piper wasn't impressed by excessive taxidermy. In her opinion, the only way hunting would be fair was if the animals had AK-47s.

"Did he bag those trophies himself?" Gavin asked.

"Yep, and Josef is real proud of his hunting skill. Claims that his son, Taimar Drako, is a better shot than he is."

"Makes you wonder…" Gavin picked up the last

of his calzone and gestured with it, causing a reaction from Izzy.

"Moof," the dog said.

After he broke off a tiny bite for Izzy, Gavin continued. "Josef's son fired two point-blank shots that didn't kill Marco. If he's as good a hunter as his dad says, Tai didn't want Marco dead."

"Just what I was thinking," DJ said. "Here's some history on Josef. Five years ago, he went through an amicable divorce. His only son, Taimar, is twenty-four. Josef's wife is from the Siletz tribe and her parents are bigwigs at two of the casinos along the coast. He has a wall filled with photos of his wife—a good-looking woman with straight black hair hanging down to her waist—and her family. They got Josef his job as a supervisory pit boss at the larger casino, which he kept even after the divorce."

"Gambling problem?" Gavin asked.

"Don't think so. I had Beekman check his credit, bank account and investments. He's mostly clean. Two arrests for drunk and disorderly, one DUI, a bunch of parking tickets and one assault charge when a bar fight got out of hand."

"Doesn't seem like he'd get tickets in Devil's Lake or near the casino. Where was Josef parking illegally?"

"Portland," DJ said. "Always the same general area. Right near his girlfriend's house, which might account for the divorce."

Finishing his second calzone, Gavin wiped his fingers and studied his fellow marshal. "I'm still waiting for the good stuff. Tell me about Yuri, the original Dragon."

"Josef claims that he's only visited the prison in Sheridan four or five times during the past six months."

"Did you verify?" Gavin asked.

"You know I did. Five visits. The last three he brought Taimar with him." DJ picked up an unused fork from the table. "Have I earned a bite?"

"Not yet."

Piper quietly observed the two marshals as they chatted back and forth like a couple of tennis players lobbing comments. Slightly older and more experienced, Gavin was the stronger, the top seed, the alpha. But DJ represented a strong contender.

Gavin took a foil-wrapped calzone from the insulated bag and held it just out of DJ's reach. "What happened when you talked to Yuri Drako in the prison?"

"I can't tell you."

"Why not?"

"Because it hasn't happened yet." He glanced down at his wristwatch. "The warden scheduled this communication in about a half hour. I thought you'd want to take part."

"Excellent." Gavin set the foil-wrapped meat pie on the table in front of DJ. "You're going to need a plate to eat that. Calzones are kind of messy."

And so is this conversation. Piper looked from one marshal to the other. Their Q and A covered a lot of territory about Josef Drako and his son but also left many issues unanswered. Did the divorce affect Taimar? How did he lose his front tooth? How did Josef feel about revenge? The fact that stood out to her was something she and Gavin had discussed before: Tai had had a clear chance to kill Marco and hadn't acted upon it. He could have also killed her and Izzy. Why didn't he? What were his instructions?

With one of the guards who had been stationed outside Marco's room in tow, Sofia dashed across the cafeteria to their table. Izzy gave a welcoming thump of her tail, and Piper gently smiled as she remembered the sweet moment when the young woman sang for her dad.

"Can you believe it?" Sofia planted her fists on her slender hips. "The nurse told me visiting hours were over. I can come back tomorrow, but no more today."

Piper thought the nurse had been a good sport, allowing them to talk to Marco and giving Sofia extra time with her father. "The doctor said your dad will be in the hospital for two or three more days to guard against infection."

"Then what?"

"I'm not sure what you mean."

"Do we go back to the house in Beaverton? Get shipped to Portland? Maybe we'll be in WITSEC in North Dakota. Will I ever see Logan again? This is so completely unfair." She slumped into a chair. Without asking for permission, she grabbed a cannoli and bit into it, creating a flurry of powdered sugar. "My life sucks."

Though Piper had chosen the same dinner, she

had a knee-jerk reaction to the teenager eating pastry instead of nourishing food. She clenched her jaw to keep from scolding. This incarnation of Sofia wasn't the same as the lovely angel who'd sang for Marco. This was Sofia the Teenaged Terror.

Gavin pushed back his chair and stood. "I'm going to find an office with some privacy for our video chat with Drako. I'll be back in a minute."

Sofia's green eyes narrowed as she watched Gavin and the bodyguard from the fifth floor walk away. "What's going on? Where are we going to sleep tonight?"

"There are several alternatives." Piper didn't think she should mention Marco's sanctuary until it was a sure thing. "Gavin hasn't told me which he thinks would be best."

"Why does he get to choose?" She leaned toward DJ. "Do you think that's fair?"

"You bet I do," he drawled. "Marshal McQueen needs to protect you, and he can't do that if you're not cooperating."

"Of course, you'd take his side. I'll forgive you if you let me use your cell phone."

"Not a chance."

She reached under the table and petted the dog. "What about you, Izzy? You're on my team, aren't you? You liked Logan when you met him. You know we should be together."

Piper doubted that Sofia would be interested in her defense of Gavin and an explanation about why the US Marshals Service couldn't care less about her budding romance with Logan. The teenager had already decided that the earth orbited around her.

GAVIN HAD TUCKED PIPER, Sofia and Izzy into an office behind the reception area where he and DJ waited to hear from the warden at the federal prison in Sheridan, a medium-security facility that was—in Gavin's opinion—too pleasant and lenient for the likes of Yuri Drako. True, the old man was ninety-six and required round-the-clock nursing care. True, he hadn't been convicted of murder, but he'd plotted to hijack an airplane—an act of domestic terrorism that had been thwarted only because of Marco's testimony. True, Yuri had less power because others had taken the reins of his crime empire. The old Dragon might seem toothless, but Gavin knew that Yuri Drako couldn't be trusted and should not, under any circumstance, be released.

DJ set up his laptop on the receptionist's desk where he sat facing a full-screen logo for the prison while they waited for the warden to open communication with Drako. Gavin had taken a position to the far left of the computer screen where Drako couldn't see him. No point in giving the old dragon more information than necessary. At some point during the interview, he might interrupt. Both he and DJ had investigative paths they'd been following.

Warden Henry Oakley appeared on the screen, introduced himself and laid out the parameters of their face-to-face conversation. "You have exactly fifteen minutes. I assume you will be recording, Marshal Johnson."

"Yes, sir," DJ said.

"Mr. Drako has agreed to the recording. He has also waived his option to have an attorney present, but he has the right—at any time—to end the interview without explanation. He appreciates this opportunity to aid in your investigation."

Gavin clenched his jaw to keep from blurting out his disgust. *What right did Drako have for laying out terms?* This career criminal had enriched himself at the expense of others. Without remorse, he'd shattered the lives of innocent people like Sofia and Marco. Instead of punishment, Drako had snagged a spot at this moderate security facility that allowed him to hire his own nurses.

"We appreciate the cooperation," DJ said. Supposedly, he was calm and reasonable, but Gavin saw the tension in DJ's shoulders. A blush crawled up his throat and turned his cheeks bright red.

Warden Oakley adjusted the position of the screen, and Gavin found himself staring into the soulless black eyes of Yuri Drako. Though he'd never met the old Dragon in person, the face was familiar. *A mask of evil.* In spite of incarceration, his olive complexion had deepened and looked like a tan. Not that he appeared to be outdoorsy or healthy. His harsh cheekbones supported a mass of wrinkles. Beneath his thick, black hair, which was combed straight back, deep crevasses carved lines across his forehead. Heavy brackets circled his thin lips. When he smiled, he displayed the finest gleaming white teeth money could buy.

"Good afternoon," Drako said to DJ in his lightly accented voice. "I was so very sorry to hear about the attack on Maxim Lombardi."

Interesting. He'd used Marco's real name.

Drako continued. "I pray for his speedy recovery. Please pass along my regrets for the pain he must be suffering."

"I sure enough will," DJ said.

"And you are Marshal Daniel Johnson," Drako said, "recently married to a lovely brunette named Chelsey."

At the sound of his wife's name, DJ stiffened. But he managed to hold it together, not responding to Drako's prod. "I learned that you and Marco have a correspondence going."

"His name is Maxim. A good Russian name given to him by his mother."

"Maxim," DJ muttered. Gavin heard the edge in his voice. "I'm curious, Mr. Drako, why did you contact Maxim?"

"Is this not obvious?" A dry laugh rattled in his throat, and he made a gesture, summoning his nurse— a stunning blonde who handed him a glass of water. When Drako resumed, he said, "There are those who would harm Maxim Lombardi and his talented daughter. I wished to warn him."

Like hell he did.

Chapter Thirteen

Though anxious to take his turn with Drako, Gavin left DJ in charge of the interview. He scribbled a note on a piece of paper and slid it across the desk toward the screen of the laptop. DJ glanced down, nodded to Gavin and spoke to Drako. "You never wanted to harm Marco and Sofia. Is that correct?"

"Da."

"Somebody else did. Why was Marco shot? Who ordered the hit?"

"Open your eyes, Marshal Johnson. Has it escaped your notice that I am incarcerated? I have no influence in your world. My only companions are my doctors and the nurses who make me comfortable. My angels." Baring his dentures in what might pass as a smile, he gestured toward the blonde who leaned close to the screen and waved. Her physical charms ranked high on the hotness meter. "Surely you don't think this lovely woman could be an assassin."

"Listen, Drako, I don't want—"

"Her name is Alexandra. And she's not married."

"But I am." DJ read the single word on Gavin's note. "Ivanov. Tell me about him."

"My old friend," Drako said with a glint in his cold, hard eyes. "I heard he engineered an escape from the penitentiary in Jersey. Very clever, don't you think?"

"Do you know his whereabouts?"

"His plans and prospects are none of my affair."

Gavin wanted to scoff, wanted to rake this old man over the coals and force him to divulge whatever scheme he and Ivanov had planned. Did it involve airplanes and hijackings like their plan six years ago in Jersey? What did Ivanov, the pilot, have up his sleeve? So many questions, but they only had fifteen minutes for this interview and their time was running out.

DJ carried on. "We're tracking Ivanov. He's making his way west, heading toward the Pacific Coast."

"I wish him well."

"He's coming to see you."

"Nyet."

Again, Gavin prompted the younger marshal by shoving the ID photo of Taimar Drako across the desktop. After a glance, DJ stared into the computer screen and said, "Your grandson."

"Taimar," Drako said, "a handsome boy with a bright future."

"Not if he follows the same path you've taken. We've identified your grandson as the shooter who attacked Marco. We're searching for him. Every law enforcement officer in the State of Oregon—from the feds to the traffic crossing guards—is on the hunt."

Drako showed neither surprise nor concern. Instead, he scoffed. "And you have witnesses, correct? A dog and a truffle hunter, Piper Comstock."

Hearing her name spoken in Drako's accented English disgusted Gavin. His words crashed like a tsunami. He wanted to reach through the laptop and strangle this pathetic son of a bitch. Instead, he tapped DJ's shoulder and asked, "May I?"

When DJ nodded, Gavin angled the screen so he looked directly into the dragon's maw. He didn't bother with introducing himself. The old man seemed well versed on their investigation. No doubt he had confidential dossiers on all of them. "You forget, Drako, that Marco Barbieri confronted your grandson. He is the primary witness. As soon as we apprehend Taimar, he will be going to jail for attempted murder."

"Not if my lawyers have anything to say about it." He frowned in fake concern. "It must have been an unfortunate accident or self-defense. I promise you, my grandson would not fail if he made such an attempt."

Gavin had more questions. He might have tried a more subtle approach, but their time was almost up. He returned to the first line of inquiry. "How long have you been speaking with Marco?"

"Maxim," he corrected. "A few weeks, perhaps a month, perhaps more."

"Why did you wait until recently to make contact?"

"I wasn't sure he'd want to hear from me."

That was the most honest statement Drako had made. Marco's testimony had put the dragon in jail but had also caused him to give up his beloved restaurant in Jersey and completely alter his lifestyle. By all logic, they ought to hate each other. "What changed your mind?"

"A man reaches a point in his life when he seeks the reassurance of old friends. When I think of Maxim, I can almost taste his delicious borscht and chicken Kiev. I have a chef here in Sheridan, but he's not as good."

"Are you telling me that, in spite of your differences, you've developed a cordial relationship?"

"We deepened our existing friendship."

"If you're such good buddies, he must tell you everything."

"Da."

Gavin hoped that Marco had been circumspect. "What do you think of his sanctuary? Pretty nice setup, isn't it?"

For an instant, Drako's smug expression vanished. "Sanctuary?"

"He must have mentioned it to you. Since you're so close."

"Da, of course. Remind me again of the location." His left eyelid twitched. "I'm an old man. I tend to forget addresses and such."

Gavin didn't buy this excuse. He'd surprised Drako with the mention of a sanctuary, which made him think that was the best place he could take Piper and Sofia. If the Dragons didn't know it existed, they couldn't find it.

"That's all for now, Drako. But we'll be in touch."

AFTER HOURS IN the vacant offices at Overton Hospital, Piper went down a narrow hallway with doors on each side and into an examination room with Gavin while DJ, Sofia and Izzy stayed in the outer office and polished off the calzones and cannolis. When Gavin closed the door to the tiny room, Piper assumed the role of doctor, gave him a clinical look and ordered, "All right, young man, take off your pants and hop up on the table."

"You first."

She was glad to see him smile. He hadn't shaved this morning and dark stubble outlined his jaw. *Sexy.* "How was your conversation with Drako?"

"Irritating as hell. He knows too much about our investigation."

Someone on the inside feeding him information? "You said there might be a rat."

"And when I find out who it is, I'll make sure he or she has a cell near Drako so they can talk to each other all the time. The old man mentioned DJ's wife and you—a witness to the shooting—by name."

A chill trickled down her spine. She was a truffle hunter with a stay-at-home business selling and designing software. Not the sort of person who had contact with an infamous crime boss. *Wrong place, wrong time.* "How did I stumble into this?"

"I mention his comment to emphasize—once

again—that the danger to you and Izzy is very real. You're on the Dragon's radar."

"How long is Drako going to be a threat?"

"Well, he's ninety-six and supposedly ill, but I wouldn't be surprised if the old man lived to be a hundred and twenty."

"In prison?" She perched on a stool where a doctor usually sat when making notes on a patient's condition. "That doesn't sound like a great life."

"He's got a beautiful nurse named Alexandra, a personal chef and round-the-clock care. Not a bad deal." Gavin sank into a chair beneath an anatomical poster of a heart with the valves, muscles, veins and arteries in shades of purple and magenta. "Drako wants more than physical satisfaction. He feeds on power, thrives on it. He wants to be free. That's why he talked to Marco and why Ivanov is headed toward the West Coast. I'm sure it's all part of a plot, but I don't know what they're thinking."

"What can we do?"

"It's your job—and Sofia's—to stay safe. That's all you need to worry about."

"Don't die? I think I can handle that," she said. "Can we go to Marco's hideout?"

"When I mentioned sanctuary, Drako didn't know what I was talking about. He hasn't heard about the secret hideaway, which means it might be a very safe place while we wait for Marco to recuperate and figure out what we need to do next."

She liked the idea, liked it a lot. Staying at a secret sanctuary sounded a hundred times better than being cramped in a hotel or—even worse—stuck in an FBI safe house with a bunch of bossy know-it-all agents. "Might be ideal, but I'm not going to count on it. I've found that when something sounds too good to be true, it usually is."

"Never look on the bright side, right?"

"Call me a realist."

"I'll need to check the location of Marco's sanctuary with Beekman and make sure there isn't a paper trail of loans and deeds that would lead to the doorstep. And my computer whiz will verify that we have no electronic signal that can be tracked. Beekman will be the only ranking marshal who knows where we are, and I trust him to keep his mouth shut."

"Does anyone other than Chef Rosa know about this place?"

"She assured me that she was the only one."

When Piper had talked with Rosa at Bella Trattoria, she'd had the sense that there might have been something deeper than friendship between he and Marco. She'd been divorced for three years, enough time for the sparks to fly between them. "Do you think he took Rosa there for a rendezvous?"

"She'd tell me, wouldn't she?"

Not if it was a secret. Piper liked the idea of Marco and Rosa sneaking off to a private place where they could be alone. "I'm certain the sanctuary isn't common knowledge."

"In any case," he said, "until I get verification from Beekman and arrange the details, don't tell Sofia. If the sanctuary works out, her attitude might improve."

Piper didn't know what to think about the talented teen whose moods shifted constantly and ranged in intensity from one to one hundred and back again. "It's hard to gauge what goes on in her head. She's devastated by her dad's condition, then she's outraged, then depressed, then excited."

"Typical teenager," Gavin said.

"Is she?"

"I come from a small family. My sisters are ten and twelve years older than me, so I was always the baby. But my oldest sister has two teenaged boys, fifteen and thirteen, and I wouldn't leave either of them alone with a loaded weapon or a wallet full of cash. They're good kids, but not great when it comes to impulse control."

Getting close to Sofia caused Piper to wonder about her hopes for someday having two children, a boy and a girl. Were all teenagers so difficult? The wonderful moments when Sofia wholeheartedly embraced her might not be worth the hours of sulking and rude outbursts? "Her only consistent focus is on the boyfriend. She wants to talk to Logan on the phone or see him or tell him where we are so he can come see her."

"No contact between them," he said. "And we won't tell Sofia about the sanctuary until we're in the car on the way to the actual location."

"Maybe a little before that so she has time to get used to the idea." She glanced up into his coffee-colored eyes and hopefully suggested, "Maybe you can tell her."

Immediately, he shook his head. "Given a choice between slashing my way through fifty miles of red tape and facing off with an angry sixteen-year-old, I'll pick the tape every time."

When she reached for the door handle, he caught her hand and turned her toward him. Surprised by the warmth of his touch, she confronted him head-on and noticed a subtle difference in his expression. His gaze sharpened. The jut of his jaw showed determination.

"When I was talking to Drako," he said, "and the evil, old dragon mentioned you by name, my gut exploded. I've never felt outrage like that before. The inside of my skull burst into a fiery red. Sounds dramatic, huh? But it was real. If Yuri Drako had been in the room, I would have killed him."

Though she couldn't look away from him, she shook her head. "That's not true."

"Yeah, it is. I know it's my job to protect you, but this overwhelming urge wasn't based on my sworn duty as a marshal. This feeling went deeper. I'd give my life for you, Piper. That's not a lie."

She opened her mouth to speak, but no words came out. She didn't understand what was happening between them. They barely knew each other. How could they so quickly reach this level of intensity? She was far too sensible to be swept off her feet.

With his free hand, he opened the door. Time to return to the real world.

The first sound she heard was Sofia's voice whining. "It's not fair. You're not fair."

Marshal DJ responded. "Nobody promised life would be fair."

"Let me use your phone for five minutes."

Izzy stood beside her, providing canine backup. The dog seemed to think Sofia could do no wrong. She gave a supportive, little bark.

"Just five minutes." Sofia held up her hand, fingers splayed. "After that, I promise I'll be quiet."

"Not going to happen," DJ said.

Piper hated to interrupt when DJ seemed to have the situation under control, but Sofia spotted her, dashed toward her and launched a more aggressive plea. "Tell him, Piper. I need to make one phone call, really need to."

"You want to call Logan?"

"Who else?" She bit her lower lip. "Puh-leeze. Don't you trust me?"

Not a bit. "I'm afraid a phone call isn't appropriate."

While she was occupied with Sofia, DJ and Gavin dodged through the glass door and escaped the reception area of the outpatient offices. Not that she and Sofia were left alone. Two officers posted at the door acted as bodyguards. Never alone, they were watched over like a couple of eggs about to hatch. Piper understood the necessity but found the constant surveillance to be insulting, as if she and Sofia and Izzy were incapable of handling themselves.

"If you were me," Sofia said, "you'd want to call the person who meant more to you than anyone else in the whole world. Wouldn't you?"

Piper refused to make that comparison. "It's not the same thing. I'm an adult who has been married, divorced, moved across the country and started a new life. You've got miles to go before you earn the right to call the shots."

"But it's my life." She threw her hands in the air. "Omigod, I can't wait to be old enough to make my own decisions. Someday, I want to live in a safe little cabin like yours and have my own life."

She has a point. Being older didn't necessarily mean wiser. Piper reconsidered. If Sofia talked to her boyfriend and didn't arrange a meeting, there wasn't a problem. What could it possibly hurt?

"Five minutes," Piper said. "And you can't make any plans with him."

"Will you be listening?" Sofia asked.

"Absolutely." She led the way to the back of the receptionist's desk and pointed to the landline. "Do it before I change my mind."

Sofia planted a kiss on Piper's cheek. "You're so much cooler than the marshals."

Or so much dumber. "Five minutes. And after this, no more whining."

She went around to the front of the desk to give Sofia a sense of privacy and listened while she crooned to Logan about how much she missed him and couldn't wait to see him. Piper was glad the conversation stayed at the PG level and the L-word wasn't used.

When time was almost up, Piper called out, "That's four minutes. One more to go. Wrap it up."

Through the glass door of the office, she saw an unfamiliar figure. He showed a badge and identification card to the officers standing guard. When they read his documents, they straightened their shoulders. For a moment, she thought they might salute.

The stranger pushed the door open. He wore the sort of perfectly fitted suit that she recognized from her days as a corporate executive. Dark gray and virgin wool, probably Tom Ford, with a blue shirt and no necktie. His shoes were Armani. His wavy brown hair showed expert styling. His vivid blue eyes and smirky grin radiated confidence.

As soon as he entered, Izzy stuck her tail in the air and leaned down on her front paws—her Downward-Facing Dog position—indicating she'd found something that smelled. It might have been the stranger's citrusy cologne or something more sinister.

Izzy growled.

Piper demanded, "Who are you?"

"Marshal Phillip Esposito from Jersey. You must be the truffle hunter."

Sofia popped up from behind the desk. And Esposito identified her. "Sofia Barbieri."

When he leaned down to pat Izzy, the dog responded with another growl. Piper trusted her dog's instincts. Marshal Phillip T. Esposito was trouble.

Chapter Fourteen

Almost midnight and still lightly raining, Gavin set out in the SUV, headed for Marco's sanctuary. He was the driver, and Piper—in the passenger seat—was the navigator. In the middle seat were two rookie marshals, Frieda Mays and Zach Smith, who Gavin couldn't help thinking of as Frick and Frack, though both the man and the woman were smart and qualified. They'd joined his team last night, flying in from the California office, and had no prior association with the Dragons, which meant they couldn't be suspected of feeding information to Yuri Drako.

In the third row of seats, Sofia and Izzy slept under a couple of blankets from the hospital. The teen was finally quiet. After she'd gotten her way and made her phone call to the boyfriend, her attitude had switched from whiny complaints to more assertive demands and references to herself as a "grown-up," as if the label gave her the right to be pushy. Instead of being pleased that they were going to a place her father had prepared especially for her, Sofia resented being stuck in the middle of nowhere.

Plus, she'd insisted they make frequent visits to her father in the hospital no matter how inconvenient. Also, most important, she'd completely rejected the possibility that she and Marco would need to move to a different WITSEC location in another part of the country. Not her. No way. She'd planted roots in Oregon with her boyfriend and her career as a pop star was about to take off.

Gavin went through a series of sharp turns, doubles back and screeching stops—maneuvers designed to shake any vehicle that might attempt to follow them into the misty night. While he drove, he considered Piper's first impression of Esposito. She hadn't liked him. Neither had Izzy. For that matter, Gavin thought the marshal from Jersey was too smug and full of himself to be a good investigator. Too bad. They had to get along.

Satisfied that their SUV wasn't being tailed, he contacted DJ on the untraceable SAT phone with a scrambled signal that Beekman had provided. Throughout their journey so far, DJ had been watching Gavin's rear.

"I appreciate your help," Gavin said, "you can drop back and leave us. If you need to make contact, go through Beekman. I'll check in with you twice a day for updates."

"My last report for today is a big fat zero. Still no sign of Taimar. No activity on his credit cards. No sighting of his motorcycle. Tomorrow, I'll go to Eugene where he went to college and look for former friends he might bunk with."

"Taimar Drako went to University of Oregon?"

"He was a star hockey player. Go Ducks."

"Good luck," Gavin said. "When you find him—"

"I'll arrest him for attempted murder. See you, man. I'm headed back to Portland. Might even catch a few hours in bed with my beautiful new wife."

Gavin wished he could wholeheartedly trust DJ, whom he'd worked with for several years, but until he identified the rat, everybody was suspect. After a few miles, he whipped a final U-turn and glanced over at Piper. "Are you ready take over as navigator and tell me where to go?"

"Don't tempt me."

"You can't be angry. I went to a lot of trouble to arrange for us to stay at Marco's sanctuary. It's hidden away in a forest. A secret place. That's the kind of stuff you like."

"A hermit like me? Is that what you're implying?"

When he turned and saw her grinning, he knew she was teasing. "Just read the directions."

"The map that Marco put together isn't exactly precise." Using the dim light from the dashboard, she squinted at the piece of paper from the "sanctuary" envelope. "He uses landmarks instead of street signs, but I'm familiar with this area. We're not far from my cabin in Yamhill."

For an instant, he wished their destination was her beloved cabin. Just him and Piper without Sofia or Frick and Frack. The dog could come. "Starting here. We're driving south on Highway 101."

"Take the first exit after we pass Crab Corner Café and go left."

Within five miles, he sighted the drive-up diner with a huge well-lit sign featuring a dancing crab waving a top hat and cane. The exit led to a two-lane road headed east, away from the coast and into the surrounding forest, somewhat of a disappointment to Gavin. His favorite part of Oregon had to be the rugged coast with lighthouses, roiling surf and massive offshore rocks. When he'd learned that the sanctuary lay in that direction, he had imagined a walk on the beach at sundown with Piper. A chance to know each other better, even though their budding relationship came with an expiration date if she opted for WITSEC.

She pointed to the right. "Turn here at the Marionberry Stand. The sign says they also have blueberries, raspberries, blackberries and gooseberries. But they're closed for the season."

"Are all of Marco's landmarks about food?"

"He's a chef," she reminded. "The next is a grove of larch. At this time of year, we're talking about a large clump of yellow trees. Take a left and keep going for six miles."

"Terrible directions," he complained. "In summer, when the needles grow back, the larches look like all the other pines."

"Which is why there's a carved sign at the front of the grove that says Golden Larch."

Each road they took was narrower and less well maintained. Gradually, they were gaining altitude.

After they crossed the bridge at Cinnamon Creek and turned at Maudie's Cookies, the coastal forest became thicker. Branches and trunks of the tall, mis-shapen trees were coated with heavy moss.

"Slow down," she said. "This last turn is nothing more than two tire tracks leading into the forest."

From the back seat, he heard Frieda aka Frick comment, "This is remote. I doubt I'd get cell service or WiFi."

"You didn't bring your phone, did you?" Gavin stared into the rearview mirror, trying to make eye contact with her. "Or any other traceable electronic device?"

"No, sir. I did as you said. I'm totally unplugged."

"Feels strange," said Zach/Frack. "I always have my phone."

"You'll get used to it," Piper said. She leaned toward the windshield and peered through the rain and the forest. "This isn't much of a road."

So far, Gavin loved their route. Marco had done a great job of finding a remote, secluded sanctuary that was—at the same time—within an hour's drive of Beaverton. The land on the driver's side of the SUV had dropped away. The two-track road was about six feet from the edge of a cliff.

He spied a small cabin nestled in a forest of pon-derosa pine and hemlock, with a covered porch in front. At first glance, he didn't see the reflection from any windows. As they got closer, he realized that heavy shutters covered the glass. The rustic ap-pearance was somewhat spoiled by a security keypad at the front door—a feature Gavin appreciated. When he parked, everybody had a comment.

Sofia, of course, thought the place was deserted and creepy. Frick and Frack opened the rear door while they enthused over the very isolated location where nobody would find them. Izzy said, "Moof."

He waited to hear Piper's comment. She turned toward him. The dome light in the SUV shone on her dark auburn hair and her blue eyes glistened. "I could live here."

"Me, too." He could live here with her and become the mate of the hermit girl. "Let's check out the inside."

Gavin's respect for Marco's planning ability increased with each new discovery. Maybe the chef had spent the last six years in WITSEC figuring out how to keep himself and those he loved safe. The keypad security at the front door wasn't state-of-the-art, but it worked. If someone tried to break in, a screech owl alarm sounded nonstop until turned off. A generator provided electricity, and fresh water came from a well. The kitchen was, of course, well stocked. They could stay here for days without leaving, especially since Piper had insisted on picking up perishable supplies such as bread, eggs and milk, before they'd left civilization.

Sofia checked out the supplies in a freestanding freezer and canned goods in a pantry. "There's not much to drink besides wine."

"Which is not for you," Piper told her. "There's only one bedroom with a queen-sized bed and a single. The three women get that space. You two guys can sleep out here on the sofas."

Getting settled didn't take long. Even Izzy—who'd immediately bounded into the forest to reconnoiter—rushed into the cabin for a solid night's sleep. While they put together their bedding, Gavin wondered again why Marco had designed this solitary sanctuary. The cabin showed signs of long-term use, which indicated that this wasn't a hideout he'd thrown together after Yuri Drako had contacted him on the phone a few weeks ago. It appeared that Marco had lived here. But Sofia didn't know anything about the place, other than it was too remote and she craved more attention than she could find in the deep, thick forest.

Piper had suggested that this cabin could be Marco's love nest. Maybe she was right.

PIPER COULDN'T SLEEP. With a heavy quilt pulled up to her chin, she lay beside Sofia on the queen-sized bed and stared up at the ceiling. Frieda was on the single. They hadn't removed the rough-hewn shutters from the windows, but there was enough space between the boards to allow a few slivers of moonlight to stretch across the walls. Tree branches rustled in the wind and scraped against the cabin. Otherwise, the forest was quiet, as though waiting for something to happen.

Marco's sanctuary reminded her of her cabin in Yamhill, which should have been comforting. A secret place, unknown to Drako and his men, where they could stay without fear of being stalked or attacked. *For how long?* Piper couldn't pretend that they'd vanished from the face of the earth. Tomorrow would come, and who could guess what another day would bring. Her future had never seemed so uncertain. Even when she'd uncoupled her marriage and fled from corporate life with her tail tucked between her legs, she hadn't been so viscerally frightened. Losing a job and a marriage couldn't compare with the threat of losing her life.

She rolled onto her side. Her situation hadn't been *all* bad. Gavin made a difference. Meeting him reminded her that she had a wider scope of possibilities than hunting for truffles with Izzy. She was attracted to him and could tell that he felt the same about her. Could they have a relationship or was she dreaming? They'd only been together for slightly more than twenty-four hours. Was she reading too much into those strange and special moments when she'd caught him watching her? Did the glow of his smile mean something more than friendship? He'd admitted to having feelings—deep feelings—for her. How deep? How important?

Only one way to find out. She had to dig, to find the truth.

Slipping out of the bed, she stuck her feet into her sneakers and grabbed a sweatshirt. When she left the bedroom and entered the front room, Izzy wiggled through the door behind her. Together, they tiptoed to the front door. A tempting aroma of coffee wafted from the attached kitchen. Someone was trying to stay awake. *Gavin.* She'd heard him volunteer for the first watch, which meant he'd be on the covered front porch.

Outside, the temperature had dipped into the forties but the rain that had plagued them had finally stopped. Gavin leaned against the corner post for the stained pine railing that wrapped around the porch. Beside him was a long-barreled rifle. He sipped coffee from a large brown mug. In his jeans, turtleneck and plaid flannel shirt, he looked more like a lumberjack than a sophisticated, Portland-based marshal who wore black leather jackets. She liked both versions, and so did Izzy, who went directly to him and nudged his thigh until he reached down and scratched between her ears.

As Piper approached, she folded her arms below her breasts and realized that she wasn't wearing a bra under her sweatshirt. Her gray sweatpants bagged at the knees and butt. Self-consciously, she poked at her dark auburn hair that fell in tangles around her face and wished that she'd at least taken a moment to apply a dab of lip gloss. Ever since she and Gavin had met, she'd been unkempt, without makeup, without anything resembling styling for her hair or her clothing—her bloody and/or borrowed outfits. Not knowing where she was or where she ought to be going. Lost, frightened, confused, and a mess. Now might not be the best time to discuss the possibility of a future relationship.

But there wasn't time to wait.

She stood opposite him and stared past his shoulder at the fresh-washed pine trees and bright red leaves of chokecherry shrubs. The cabin rested on a ledge, giving a view above the wall of trees. The night sky sparkled with stars and glowed in the moonlight.

"I couldn't sleep."

"Your mind is racing," he said. "Mine, too."

"How do you get yourself to relax?"

"Some people meditate. Some sleep. Some drink." His dark-eyed gaze met hers. The glow of moonlight outlined his cheekbones and the sharp line of his jaw. "As for me, I just keep going. One step at a time."

He made his process sound simple, but she knew better. Constant decisions needed to be made. Plans had to be laid out, analyzed and enacted...or discarded. "So many things to consider."

"Not so much. It's only been twenty-eight hours since Marco was shot."

"Only a day. An intense, life-changing day." There were so many things she wanted to say. None felt smart or appropriate.

"Tell me more about when you met Marshal Esposito from Jersey."

"Izzy doesn't like him."

Gavin asked, "And what do *you* think?"

"Snappy dresser, but his superior attitude irritated me."

"Esposito has a big rep," he said. "He's like one of

those movie marshals who always get their man. He's after Ivanov the pilot."

"And DJ is after Tai," she said. "And you?"

"I'm coordinating and keeping you and the Barbieris safe. If you ask me, I've got the best assignment."

She moved to the railing and stood beside him. The aroma of his coffee mingled with a wintergreen scent that she'd come to associate with Gavin. Whether a shampoo or an aftershave, she liked the fresh smell. Though she wanted to talk about them and the relationship that had developed in the past twenty-eight hours, she returned to his investigation, a potentially less devastating topic. "What has Esposito uncovered so far?"

"Ivanov has connections across the county, and they're helping him go from airfield to airfield. Esposito interrogated a few of his contacts who, of course, claim they know nothing about illegal activities."

"As if they weren't aware that Ivanov is an escaped convict?"

"Not that they'll admit. A guy with a dragon tattoo that went up one arm and down the other claimed he knew nothing about Drako or Ivanov or anything else. His dragon ink is just a coincidence."

"Not real bright," she said. "Did Esposito say anything about motive? Why is Ivanov coming to Oregon?"

"He thinks Ivanov is coming here to help Drako get out of jail. Maybe to arrange an escape. Maybe to work a deal."

Rescuing a convicted felon in his nineties who was in poor health seemed like an improbable goal, but she recalled what Gavin had said about how Drako thrived on power. No doubt, if he were free, he'd undertake more terrible schemes, and the Dragons would follow their leader. "None of this makes sense."

"Because you don't think like a criminal. Be glad you don't understand."

"This sort of thing probably isn't as complicated and dramatic for you. I mean you're a marshal. You do this stuff every day. It's your job to carry a gun and arrest the bad guys."

"There's something different about this case."

"Because you know Marco and Sofia so well?" she asked.

"Because I met you."

With his free hand, he reached out to her. Gently, he cupped her chin and tilted her face toward him. Her heart skipped a beat. For a moment, her breath caught in her throat. *Is this really happening?* When his mouth pressed against hers, she accepted this amazing reality.

Heat spread through her body. Somehow, he'd set down his coffee mug. They were standing, locked in an embrace. Her body fit neatly against his muscular chest. Her legs twined with his.

He nibbled at her earlobe, sending an electric thrill down her neck to her spine and throughout her nervous system. He whispered, "I never want this to end."

Her lips parted for another kiss and she welcomed his tongue into her mouth. Her doubts and questions dissipated like the rains of winter. They hadn't made a commitment. For now, this kiss would have to be enough.

Chapter Fifteen

In usual circumstances, Gavin woke with a burst of energy and his senses sharp. Being alert was easy after six or seven hours of sleep. He'd barely gotten four after Piper visited him on the porch. Though his brain was still sluggish, he had no doubt that their kiss last night was the absolute right thing to do—impulsive and unprofessional but right. Until last night, he hadn't believed in love at first sight. Never expected romance to sneak up on a guy like him.

Aware of another presence, he rolled over on the sofa in the front room and pried one eye open. The face he confronted was furry.

"Moof," Izzy said.

More well behaved than most mutts, she didn't pounce and demand attention. She kept her nose eight inches away from his while she wiggled and whipped her tail back and forth. "Where's your boss?" he mumbled to the dog. "Where's Piper?"

"Did I hear my name?" She swept into the room, sat on the sturdy pine coffee table and leaned over so she was eye level with him. "Hungry?"

"Coffee."

She looked good this morning, had taken time to run a brush through her wavy shoulder-length auburn hair and dab on a bit of lipstick. A fresh blue blouse emphasized her eye color, and she'd used mascara on her naturally thick lashes. "Sofia is making breakfast from the food in the pantry and freezer. Steak and eggs with a side of grits. It looks really good."

"I'm shocked."

"Why? Her father is a chef. I'm sure she knows how to cook."

He didn't question her ability. "I didn't think she liked us well enough to care whether we ate or not."

"You might be surprised."

He'd been working with Sofia and Marco for six years and had seen the young woman through early adolescence, a first crush, and a shoplifting incident. Gavin knew she was capable of being pleasant, but he'd also encountered the monster below the adorable surface. "She doesn't surprise me," he said. "The trick is to be ready for whatever she's going to do next."

"This morning, it's breakfast."

He crawled out from under the blanket and shuffled to the one bathroom in the cabin. Unsure of how much hot water was available, he decided not to shower or shave until they got into town this morning. He'd use facilities in the hospital. Yesterday, he'd arranged to meet there with Esposito and DJ near lunchtime.

After splashing water on his face, he joined Sofia, Piper and Frieda at a long table that had been pushed up against the wall. Frieda's partner was outside, patrolling the grounds. Though Gavin felt confident that the SAT phone from Beekman was untraceable, he couldn't take a chance on being wrong and getting caught in an ambush.

Breakfast—especially the well-seasoned grits—tasted fantastic. He complimented Sofia. "Great job."

"Not so hard." She shrugged. "I know my dad's flavor profiles. The meat in the freezer is high quality, and I did a quick thaw and marinade last night."

"You're very talented," Frieda said.

"Thanks, but cooking isn't in my future. I'm a singer."

Piper added, "She's musically talented. Thousands of people saw her and liked her on social media networks."

"Someday," Sofia said as she pinned Gavin with an edgy glare, "I'm moving to New York City or La La Land and launching my career."

No comment. He cut off another piece of his perfectly seared steak and chewed, refusing to be drawn into a confrontation so early in the morning. His brain wasn't alert enough to square off with Sofia. All he wanted to do was close his eyes and relive the kiss he'd shared with Piper.

"What's the plan for the day?" Frieda asked.

"We'll go to the hospital to check on Marco at lunchtime. Then we return here."

"That doesn't work for me," Sofia said archly. "I want to stay in town. I can find my own place to spend the night."

He sipped his coffee. *Delicious.* "You'll come with us."

"You can't order me around, McQueen. You're not the boss of me."

"Yeah, I am. You're a minor, and your dad has left you in my care."

"You make me so mad. I can't even look at you." She pushed away from the table and paced. "How about if we all stay in town tonight?"

"At the FBI safe house?"

"Yuck, no. Anyplace else. I need to be somewhere that isn't the middle of nowhere."

"So you want to sleep at a cheesy motel."

"I'm trying really, really hard to be grown-up and cooperate, but you're making it impossible. What if I talk to my dad, and he says it's okay for me to stay in Beaverton?"

"Not a great idea," Piper said. "Marco should concentrate on his recovery. He doesn't need to be worrying about your safety."

Sofia stomped away from the table to the front door. "Of course, you'd take McQueen's side. You don't even care about me."

Gavin would have followed her to keep watch, but Izzy accompanied the teen. He trusted the dog to let them know if Sofia was in trouble. Protecting someone who couldn't stand the sight of you wasn't easy.

BACK AT OVERTON HOSPITAL, Gavin dropped Sofia, Piper and Izzy off to visit Marco, who felt better but was exhausted. The docs doubted he'd be released for another couple of days. Even then, he should take it easy. Not the best time to plan a WITSEC move across the country.

Gavin had arranged to use a small conference room on the fourth floor. The rainclouds hadn't reappeared and the window offered a spectacular view of Beaverton—a city with more trees than people and autumn colors in full array. Using his regular phone, he took a call from DJ, who was stuck in Eugene, tracking down Taimar Drako's former buddies. Taimar's Russian pedigree had enhanced his standing on the hockey team. Though he wasn't a huge guy, he'd played power forward, got his tooth knocked out, engaged in plenty of battles against the boards and spent a lot of time in the penalty box.

"Too aggressive," DJ said. "Not popular. I talked to a roommate who lived with Tai for a couple of months and told me he was a rich kid with a nasty temper."

"Has Tai been in contact with any of them?"

"Not recently."

"Girlfriends?"

"That's my best lead," DJ said. "I'm trying to reach a young woman who graduated last year and got a job in Portland. Thought I'd catch her at work this afternoon when I go home."

"Keep at it," Gavin said. "Let me know if there's anything I can do to help."

Much of investigative work involved the routine tracking down of one clue after another until something popped. DJ had the necessary patience and a fine-tuned sense of when people were lying or holding back information. He was also a team player, freely sharing ideas and opinions. Gavin liked working with the husky, blond guy and truly hoped he wouldn't turn out to be the rat.

Not like Esposito, who arrived at the conference room a full half hour later than they'd agreed upon. Typically, the marshal from Jersey worked alone, specializing in apprehending escaped felons. He'd made it clear from the start that Gavin wasn't his superior, which had never been Gavin's intention. He merely wanted to help, to put Esposito in touch with people who might make his investigation into tracking Tom Ivanov easier and to navigate the local logistics. Oregon was different from New Jersey, and sometimes it was handy to have a tour guide.

Esposito had changed from his virgin wool suit into what he must have considered "Western" wear. With his brand-new denim jacket, jeans with a crease down the front, and fancy, lizard-skin, pointy-toed cowboy boots, he was a walking definition of a greenhorn…though still carrying a leather briefcase. A gleaming white ten-gallon hat covered his perfectly trimmed brown hair.

Gingerly, he lowered himself into a chair at the conference room table. "I don't know how you people walk around in these boots."

"We don't." Gavin leaned back in his chair and rested his feet on the table. "These are hiking boots. Comfortable, waterproof, and ample protection from stickers and ankle-biting critters."

"Where do I find decent shoes?"

"Just about any place," Gavin said as he lowered his feet. "Make sure they're waterproof. We're into the rainy season."

Esposito opened his briefcase and took out the skinniest laptop Gavin had ever seen. It powered up with the touch of a button. A map of the area surrounding the penitentiary in Sheridan appeared on the screen. Four red circles marked places of interest. "I'm going to need backup at one or more of these locations."

"When?"

"Not today. Tomorrow or the next day."

"And what are these sites?"

"Airfields, places where a small plane can land."

Gavin wasn't sure whether Esposito was withholding information on purpose to make him dig for it or just wasn't accustomed to communicating to others. "What do you expect will happen at one of these airfields?"

Esposito lifted his chin and aimed his sharp, intense gaze directly at Gavin. "Hostage exchange," he said.

LATER IN THE AFTERNOON, Piper wanted to trek into the thick pine, cedar and hemlock forest surrounding the sanctuary to arrange a truffle search. Izzy was restless after a day spent in the SUV and at the hospital. The mutt needed a chance to get out and run around. The same was true for Sofia, who hadn't gotten over her argument with Gavin this morning. Before leaving the cabin, Piper invited her to come along.

"Not interested," Sofia said in clipped tones.

"It'll be good for you to be outdoors. Get some fresh air."

Nervously, she twisted her long hair around her index finger. "Whatever happens, Piper, I want you to know. It's not your fault."

Weird comment. "What do you expect to happen?"

"Nothing. Just forget it."

"We'll be back in half an hour or so. Then, dinner."

Taking Gavin by the hand, Piper set out for the forested area. Izzy bounded along beside them, sniffing every leaf, splashing through a narrow creek, happily chasing the chipmunks and ground squirrels. "I was out here earlier," she said, "and I planted three small truffles from those I gave to Chef Rosa at Bella Trattoria. They're hidden at the roots of trees where they're usually found. This way Izzy is guaranteed to get a hit."

When she glanced over at him, he seemed preoccupied. She added, "Hiding the truffles probably doesn't seem fair, but Izzy gets depressed if she fails. Don't we all?"

Ten yards away from the cabin, they disappeared into the trees. He halted, held her upper arms and turned her toward him. "I'm glad we're here. I needed to get you alone."

"I'm flattered." She jumped to the happy conclusion that he was interested in another kiss. "We'll have time for that later. Right now, let's concentrate on Izzy and the truffles."

"Esposito knows what Ivanov has planned."

An enormous revelation. If they had advance warning, they could prepare. "How did he find out? Did he talk directly to Ivanov?"

"Second-best thing. Esposito has a confidential informant, another pilot. This guy has done work for the Dragons before."

She didn't want to be suspicious. Piper preferred to believe everything she heard but being gullible could get you into trouble. "Can this informant be trusted?"

"Esposito believes him."

"But do we believe Esposito?" She thought of the rat, the inside person who had been feeding information to Drako. Her opinion of the marshal from Jersey wasn't positive. And Izzy didn't like him.

"We can't be sure of anything," Gavin said, "but this plot has credibility, given the way the Dragons do business. Drako likes to make a big gesture, something to capture headlines. This might be it."

Izzy bounced up to them, expecting to get started on the truffle hunt. She looked from Gavin to Piper and back again. Piper knelt to scratch behind Izzy's ears. "Don't worry, girl. I won't forget the real reason we're outdoors."

Obediently, Izzy sat. Both the dog and Piper turned to Gavin. "Tell us."

"Six years ago, the plan engineered by Drako was to highjack an airliner and use the passengers in a hostage exchange to free their comrades from jail. Ivanov's current scheme uses the same principles. Only he's downsized."

"Smaller plane?" she guessed.

"And fewer hostages." His forehead wrinkled in a frown, and she knew there was more—much more—he needed to tell her. "He'll contact Esposito and arrange a meet at an airfield near the penitentiary in Sheridan. Yuri Drako will be traded for the hostages."

Simple. Though it seemed selfish to think only of herself, Ivanov's plan solved many of their problems. "I guess there's nothing we can do but sit tight and wait for it to happen. We're not in danger, are we?"

"Here's where it gets sticky."

Horrendous complications raced through her mind. She didn't know what to expect. The possibilities were endless…and terrifying. "Tell me."

"Remember when I talked about revenge?"

"Of course, but what does that have to do with…" A terrible conclusion formed in her mind. She couldn't believe it, didn't want to believe it.

"Marco and Sofia," Gavin said. "He wants to use them as hostages."

No, no, no, no, this could not be. "Drako's revenge."

"When Tai came to Marco's house, he wasn't supposed to shoot the old man. He was there to pick him and Sofia up and take them to a hideout near his father's house in Devil's Lake. Drako thought he'd convinced Marco to go along with his plan."

"But he was wrong. Marco would never put his daughter in danger." The old chef had created this entire sanctuary to keep Sofia safe. "What should we do? Is it safe to stay here?"

"I'm thinking we ought to hook up with the FBI and surround Sofia with special agents," he said. "This hideout is great, but you and me and Frick and Frack aren't an unstoppable force if Ivanov somehow locates us. We'll leave after dark. Sofia's not going to like it."

"There isn't much that makes her happy. Only Logan." Piper straightened her shoulders. "For now, we hunt."

In spite of her fear and tension, she keyed her voice to a light, playful tone while she told Izzy what a wonderful mutt she was, how beautiful and smart.

At first, Izzy wasn't buying the happy talk. She knew Piper well enough to sense her mood. The dog sat back on her haunches and scratched behind her ear.

"What's the matter, girl?"

"Moof," Izzy said.

"I don't get it," Gavin said. "This doesn't look like hunting."

Piper reached into her jacket pocket, took out a resealable plastic bag filled with doggy treats and gave one to Izzy. "I communicate with Izzy through tone of voice and meaty treats. If I'm cheerful and encouraging, she'll respond."

She chatted with Izzy about the sunny skies and the wonderful thick forest. Then she straightened and issued a command in a more authoritative tone. "Seek and find, Izzy. Get the truffles. Seek."

Izzy bobbed her head as though she understood exactly what Piper was saying. Then she took off, dodging through the forest, going from tree to tree.

Trailing behind Izzy's wagging tail, Piper repeated the commands. She glanced at Gavin. "This shouldn't take long. As soon as we're finished with our hunt, we can concentrate on taking Sofia into town and surrounding her with bodyguards."

"Why can't we leave now?"

"It's all about the truffles. These are pricey little mushrooms. I've got probably seventy-five bucks strewn around out here, and I'd like to clean up."

"No problem."

"Are you sure? I'll be glad to go if you think it's necessary." She wasn't going to be comfortable until Sofia was locked away in a safe house. "Seek and find, Izzy."

The half-poodle, half-shepherd zeroed in on one of the trees where Piper had earlier hidden the truffle. Izzy pawed at the soil near the root of the cedar tree, then she took her Downward-Facing Dog position with her tail in the air like a flag.

After distracting Izzy with a treat, Piper went to her knees and hovered over the spot Izzy indicated. Using a small, specialized trowel and her gloved hands, Piper pushed away the dirt covering the surface. "The first truffle hunters—and possibly the best—were pigs. They're great at locating truffles because they love to eat them. Their taste for truffles became a problem. The pig would often eat the treasure they uncovered before it could be removed and cleaned."

Instead of rushing her, Gavin knelt beside her to watch. "Can I do the next one?"

"Shouldn't we hurry?"

"A few minutes more or less shouldn't be a problem."

She knew he was wrong when Frick and Frack burst into the forest behind them. Frack's cheeks were bright red and he was gasping for breath. "Sofia. She's gone."

Chapter Sixteen

"Was she kidnapped?" Gavin's voice deepened to a growl as he questioned the rookie marshals from California. "Did someone capture her?"

"No, sir," Zach said. "She took off on her own."

"She left a note on the kitchen counter," Frieda added. "An explanation."

"On her own? On purpose?"

"I was keeping watch on the porch," Zach said. "I don't know how she got past me."

By sneaking out a back window. Gavin couldn't believe he'd thought a couple of urban-based newbies could stand watch in Oregon's forests, but he wasn't going to waste time yelling at them. He was in charge; this was his fault.

Gritting his teeth, he held back his anger. First, he raged at himself for not anticipating this move on Sofia's part. He should have known she'd pull something, should have stopped her. Second, he cursed the WITSEC program that caused this teenager to deny her dreams and hopes. Finally, he swore—still in silence—at Sofia for being a brat. How the hell could she run off? Didn't she know that she was putting herself in danger? Of all the unthinking, inconsiderate, childish—

He stopped himself before he went any further. If anything had happened to this brat—this young woman who thought of no one but herself—his heart would break. Sure, Sofia drove him to his wit's end, but he cared about her with a love that went high as the moon and deep as the Mariana Trench. *I've got to find her.*

Pulling himself together, he held out his hand. "The note. Let me see the note she left."

Frieda handed over a piece of pink stationary with an ornate *S* for Sofia centered at the top—an odd item to pack in her go-bag but he didn't understand how her mind worked.

He read loudly enough that Piper could hear. "'Don't be mad, you guys. I need to take control of my life. I called Logan from the hospital this morning and arranged to meet. I cannot believe I used landlines twice in two days. ASAP, I plan to buy a prepaid phone. I have cash, always pack a wad in my go-bag. I'll call. Don't worry. *DON'T TELL DAD.* Love, Sofia.'"

Piper sniffled. A tear crept down her cheek.

Beside her, Izzy was silent. No friendly "moof" noises. No wagging of her tail. The mutt raised her eyebrows and looked nervous.

"We're all worried," Gavin said. Especially now that he knew Ivanov intended to kidnap Sofia and use her as a hostage. "It won't do any good to sit around and mope. Frieda and Zach, I doubt you'll be able to track Sofia—the kid knows her way around a forest—but I want you to search in all directions and figure out where Logan parked. Last time we saw him, he drove a Chevy truck."

"Big enough to haul goats," Piper added.

"But he has access to other vehicles. Find the tire tracks. We need a starting point." He gestured to Piper. "Come inside with me. I need a make a few calls."

She balked. "Do you mind if I get my truffles first?"

She was unbelievable, and—much as he hated to admit it—kind of adorable with her intense focus on a stinky mushroom. "Hurry."

Instead of going inside, he went to the front of the sanctuary and stood on the cliff at the edge of the retaining wall where he gazed into a blue sky with a light haze of clouds. The forested landscape spread for miles without a soul in sight. He couldn't see all the way to the coast but spied a perfectly still lake that reflected the trees with the clarity of a mirror. The serenity should have soothed him, but Gavin felt the ragged edge of panic slashing like a chainsaw within him.

Using his SAT phone, he put in a call to Marshal Johnson who hadn't been at the meeting with Esposito where he'd talked about the hostage exchange. So much was happening so fast. Gavin had some serious explaining to do before he dropped the bombshell and told DJ that Sofia was MIA.

When DJ answered, Gavin asked, "Where are you?"

"Portland. I just talked to Taimar Drako's former girlfriend, Sarah Desmond. She saw him last night. He stopped by the shop where she's working this summer and wanted her to come with him. He was driving the forest-green Hummer I saw at his father's place."

"He had the option of driving that car and instead took a little motorcycle." Gavin shook his head in disbelief. "This kid isn't too smart."

"Gets worse for Tai. The girlfriend wasn't impressed enough by his Hummer to go for a ride, which is good news for us. Won't be hard to check his dad's license plate, and there aren't all that many Hummers on the road."

"Find a place to sit and listen," Gavin said. "I've got a long story to tell you."

While he talked to DJ, he watched Piper moving through the trees with Izzy at her side. Unlike Frick and Frack, she moved like a graceful wood nymph, dodging around thick shrubs and instinctively ducking her head to avoid having her ponytail tangled in spiky pine branches. He knew she was upset by Sofia's rebellious stunt, worried that the teenager had stumbled into waters that were too deep, but Piper—much like him—didn't allow her panic to show. She kept herself in control, tried to be useful.

When he wrapped up his report about Esposito's inside information, DJ interrupted. "He claims to have learned all this from an informant, right?"

"That's his story." Gavin knew what DJ would say next. "You're wondering if our friend from New Jersey has a closer connection to Drako."

"When we talked to Yuri Drako, he knew too much for a man who has been incarcerated for six years. Somebody on the inside might have been talking to him, and I'm guessing that a guy with a rep like Esposito has heavy experience with undercover work, playing one side against the other."

Though Gavin wouldn't put it past Esposito to exchange info with Yuri in the hope that he could catch a high-profile escaped prisoner like Ivanov, he hadn't gotten that vibe. "It's possible. I don't know."

"Considering your years with WITSEC," DJ said, "you still haven't learned some of the basics. You're not good at picking up when somebody is lying."

"You don't know how right you are." Gavin paced to the porch and sat on the stairs beside the railing. "I just got played by a sixteen-year-old. Sofia arranged to meet her boyfriend and took off."

"You lost her?"

Gavin flinched. "It appears so."

Under his breath, DJ muttered a few choice curses. "What do we do next?"

"Logan won't hurt her on purpose, but what's he going to do if Ivanov finds them?" He hated to imagine the outdoorsy young man with blond hair flopping over his forehead matched against Ivanov—a cold, sinister felon who had committed more than one murder. "I'd feel better if Sofia was protected by professionals, like you or me."

"Damn straight." Gavin could almost see DJ puffing out his chest. "We've got the guns. We've got the training. We're US Marshals, and we're good at what we do."

"Since you're already in Portland," Gavin said, "put out a BOLO on Logan Offenbach and Sofia, include license plates for any vehicles he or his mother might own. I'm headed to the commune where Logan lives, and I'll check other places he and Sofia might hang out."

"Dmitri and his two comrades are still in jail in Beaverton," DJ said. "I know because the local cops contacted me and want to know about the charges. Right now, we're holding them on vehicular violations for the chase, but we're going to need more to keep those boys locked up."

Gavin had almost forgotten about Dmitri, a punk who was, no doubt, a very small fish in a very big pond. Still, little fish could be poisonous. Dmitri and his friends had caused plenty of trouble by aiding and abetting Taimar. There could be other infractions.

"Here's my advice: Hand those wannabe Dragons off to the feds and let them prosecute."

"Seriously? The feds?"

Gavin liked the idea of getting Dmitri and whatever mischief he had planned shifted to another branch of law enforcement. The FBI had more agents and more resources. "Matter of fact, you ought to check in at FBI headquarters in Portland and at their safe house. We need to start sharing intel. If Ivanov hijacks a plane, federal agents are going to be involved."

DJ's gung-ho excitement lowered a few notches. "I'm going to need backup."

"You're right about that. Esposito has five potential locations for the hostage exchange. I think you should handle the logistics."

"Esposito, huh? Not sure I should be working with him. What if he's dirty?"

"Use your own judgment. You know the procedures for internal investigations."

"Don't like those investigations."

Nobody wanted to point the finger. None of the marshals or anybody in law enforcement wanted to believe their coworkers were untrustworthy. Temptation was rampant. They regularly dealt with millionaire criminals who offered massive payoffs. Not to mention the rewards that came from associating with wealthy, important people. "You'll know the right thing to do."

"I'm a team player," DJ said, "not a supervisor. I've never done anything this complicated before."

Gavin glanced over at Piper and Izzy as they quietly joined him on the porch stairs between the railings. They were his priority: the woman he was beginning to care deeply about and her dog. And, of course, Sofia and Marco. Gavin wanted to devote all his time and energy to protecting his witnesses.

The advice he offered DJ applied to himself, as well. "You'll catch on. There's no time like the present to learn."

"You're saying that I'm in charge?"

"It's all up to you, Marshal Johnson." In a way, this was a sort of promotion, an opportunity for DJ to make his new wife proud. Gavin probably should have gone through proper channels, consulting with his supervisor and the supervisor above him, but he wanted to get this investigation moving. "Esposito suspects the hostage exchange will go down tomorrow or the next day."

"I'm on it," DJ said with a renewed burst of enthusiasm. "Happy hunting."

Gavin ended the call and turned to Piper. The worry lines across her forehead and at the corners of her cobalt-blue eyes made her features interesting and authentic in a way that was so dramatically real it took his breath away. Her honesty shone through. She didn't hide her feelings behind a mask of paint and makeup. He could clearly see her frustration and her fear. "We'll find Sofia."

"I don't know how much help I'll be. I've never handled a gun. I'm not a tracker. And my only reference for hand-to-hand combat is yoga and tai chi."

"Which aren't lethal martial arts."

"But great for flexibility," she said. "What I'm trying to say is that I'm not good in a fight, but I want to come with you to search for Sofia."

"And I want you at my side." He pushed a hank of auburn hair off her forehead and tucked it behind her ear. "Bringing you along goes against regulations, but I've probably already broken enough rules to get fired or earn a serious demotion."

"I'm sorry, Gavin."

"Don't be. I'm exactly where I want to be. Here with you is the right place at the right time."

He sealed his commitment with a gentle kiss that was clearly not enough for Piper. She surged forward, threw herself into his chest and pressed her mouth against his, demanding his complete attention. He toppled backward into the railing, wrapped his arms around her and lifted them both to their feet.

Though his top choice would be to spend the day and the night—especially the night—with her, they had other desperate concerns. "I don't want to go."

"Me, neither."

"But we've got to hurry."

"Yes."

Izzy said, "Moof."

WHILE GAVIN DROVE back to Overton Hospital in Beaverton, Piper perched at the edge of the passenger seat, straining forward against her seat belt and wishing the SUV could fly. She searched her memory, weighed every conversation she'd ever had with Sofia. Somewhere in that cascade of words, there must be a clue. A place that was special to her and Logan. Maybe the shop where they had their first kiss. They'd spent an entire day together from dawn to dusk at the shore: Cannon Beach, Seaside, Otter Rock. Where would Sofia feel safe?

In the middle seat, Frieda and Zach whispered to each other. No doubt, they were sharing the blame and feeling guilty. She watched the play of emotion on Gavin's face when he caught sight of them in his rearview mirror. He went from angry to sad to sympathetic, and she was amazed at how easily she could read his mood.

"Any ideas?" he asked the marshals he'd referred to as Frick and Frack.

"We could requisition a chopper," Zach said. "But the forests are so thick, they probably wouldn't make a sighting."

"And Sofia doesn't want to be found," Frieda said. "She'd hide."

"What about a search and rescue dog?" Zach asked.

"Like Izzy," Piper said.

From the far back of the SUV, Izzy whapped her tail against the seat to confirm her SAR credentials.

Piper continued. "If she's going to be effective, we need a starting point. I can't just tell her to search the entire state."

"Keep thinking," Gavin encouraged. "After I drop you at the hospital, you need to approach everyone who was on duty today or yesterday—the nurses, the marshals and other law enforcement. Ask if they talked to Sofia. Did she say anything about a place she'd like to go? Take statements. Find out if they've seen Logan."

"Yes, sir." Frieda sounded glad to have an assignment. "What should we tell people, you know, about Sofia?"

"It's best to keep that information to ourselves," Gavin said.

"Right," Zach said. "There are people—like the Dragons—who don't need to know she's out there, unprotected."

"While you're at the hospital," Gavin said, "talk to Marco about his sanctuary and how it's so perfectly hidden and well supplied. Let him know his efforts are appreciated, but make sure he doesn't find out Sofia took off."

Piper backed him up. "If he knows his daughter is vulnerable, it'll take more than a doctor's order to keep him in bed."

"For everything else," Gavin said, "refer to DJ in the Portland office. He's aware of the Sofia situation."

The drive was less than an hour, but time moved as slowly as a glacier. Fidgeting, Piper checked the dashboard digital clock every few minutes, tapped her fingers on her thighs and tried deep breathing to calm her nerves. She stared through the windshield. The late-afternoon skies remained relatively clear, and the wisps of clouds surrounding Mount Hood took on a deep crimson glow against the golden sunset. "Red sky at night is a sailor's delight. That means good luck."

"If you're a fisherman," Gavin said.

Good luck. She clung to that hope with a white-knuckle grip.

A block away from the hospital, Gavin pulled to the curb and let the rookie marshals out. He didn't want anyone to see them and raise questions about Sofia's whereabouts. When he merged back into traffic and took the now-familiar route to the Offenbach commune, Izzy scooted into the second seat and got into her favorite position with her front paws on the center console.

"Do you think we should call Chris and tell her we're on our way?" Piper asked. "She'll help us, I know she will."

"Can she be trusted? The woman who sheltered Dmitri and his friends?"

"She was on the verge of kicking them out." *Does everybody have to be a suspect?* "She knew they were bad apples and didn't want her son involved with them."

He nodded in agreement but didn't change his mind. "I'd rather appear unannounced."

The constant pressure of rush-hour traffic exacerbated Piper's tension. Why was everybody going so slow and getting in the way? But when they turned onto the less traveled roads leading to the sixty-acre commune, her stress level didn't drop the way it usually did when she left the hustle and bustle. She sensed trouble ahead.

The entrance to the commune was open at this hour when many of the residents were coming home from work, and Gavin guided the SUV inside without problem or question. She noticed that most of the residents were average-looking Oregonians, some in suits, others in casual attire, and others dressed more like farmers. As Gavin drove around the landscaped central area with the gazebo-styled bandstand, she watched for signs of hostility. When people met her gaze, most of them gave her a friendly wave. Not a cult, this appeared to be a pleasant place to live.

Gavin parked outside the two-story house where spikey-haired Chris rose from one of the Adirondack chairs and came toward them. The atmosphere was almost too calm. Too perfect. Something had to pop.

She heard a low, angry rumble. Izzy was growling.

Gavin squinted at the small cedar houses to the right where Dmitri and his friends had lived. Parked in a driveway between the houses was a forest-green Hummer. Gavin rested his hand on his holstered Beretta. "He's here," he said. "Taimar Drako is here."

Chapter Seventeen

Tai couldn't believe his good fortune. That black SUV belonged to one of the marshals, probably Gavin McQueen, the guy who gave his grandpa so much trouble. Wherever the marshal went, the witness followed. And her damn dog, too. Through the SUV's dark-tinted windows, he couldn't tell how many other people were inside the vehicle, but he hoped to find Sofia. She was the one Ivanov wanted as a hostage.

From his vantage point on the roof of the Offenbach house between one of the gables and an overhanging limb of a towering ponderosa pine, he watched as Chris came down from the wraparound front porch and approached the driver's side of the SUV. She was a busybody, a troublemaker. Because of her, Dmitri and his buddies got arrested.

Tai had outsmarted Chris time after time. He'd located this hidden-in-plain-sight vantage point the first day he'd been at the commune. Walked right through the front door of her house and climbed the staircase. Nobody bothered to lock up out here.

Idiots! He'd gone out a window onto the roof. Nobody ever looked up, nobody noticed. He'd stayed for hours, looking down at the farmers go about their daily chores. He'd never get stuck in that kind of dull routine, day after day, season after season. Tai was better than that. He was a leader like his grandpa. When Yuri got out of prison, the grandson would take his rightful place, sitting at the right of the Dragon's throne.

Silent and unmoving, he peered through the scope attached to his rifle—a stun gun, not a lethal weapon. He watched McQueen, the witness and the mutt leave their SUV and rush into the house. *No Sofia.*

His instructions were to contact Ivanov with information on the hostages, but Tai wanted to prove himself. After he'd accidentally shot that stupid chef, nobody trusted him. Not even his own father who kept bugging him to get a job. If he could catch Sofia and bring her to Ivanov, he'd not only be forgiven but celebrated. In no time, the Dragons would answer to him.

He lowered his rifle and patted the holster attached to his belt. No more sissy .25-caliber handgun for him. He'd taken a semiautomatic Glock 13—a slick, deadly weapon that matched the one he'd lost at Marco's house—from his dad's gun cabinet, which had been locked. As if Tai didn't know the combination? Then he'd swiped Daddy's Hummer EV.

Tai had the equipment and the guts to pull this off. All he needed to do was to get the witness alone. She'd know where Sofia was hiding. And Tai would make her tell him. He wouldn't hurt her too much, just enough for her to know that he was the boss. He deserved payback for the way she and her dog had disarmed him.

With the stun gun rifle slung across his shoulder by a leather strap, Tai climbed back through the dormer window into the house. Before he got to Piper, he'd have to get her dog out of the way. Which would hurt worse? A bullet or 750K volts from the stun gun? Might be too much. Might kill the animal.

GAVIN KNEW TAI was near. But how close? He could be anywhere from the barn to the forest to the bandstand in the town square. Gavin figured it was a good bet that the kid had weapons. He and his dad were hunters who prided themselves on being sharpshooters. Since Tai had gone to his father's house to get the Hummer, he probably armed himself.

He hustled Piper, Izzy and Chris through the house and into the study that, if he recalled the floor plan to the house correctly, was one of the few rooms with only one door from the hallway. In here, Tai couldn't ambush them by coming through a secondary access point.

"Taimar Drako is at the commune," Gavin said as he pulled down the shade on the narrow window behind the desk. "I saw his Hummer parked at the house where Dmitri used to live."

"I don't understand," Chris said.

"Tai is trouble. This would be a good time to call the local police."

She glanced between him and Piper while she stroked Izzy's curly brown-and-black fur. "I never was introduced to him, but he seems harmless. Just a typical young man with too much time on his hands. Why is he such a big deal?"

"He shot Sofia's father," Piper said. "And he's after her."

The petting stopped, and Izzy nudged close to the short woman. The dog's nose was as high as Chris's waist. "He wants to hurt Sofia? But why?"

"It's complicated." Piper placed a comforting hand on the older woman's shoulder. "Marshal McQueen was protecting Sofia, but now she's run off with your son."

"Is Logan in danger?"

"I'm afraid so."

"Oh, no, this can't be." Chris covered her face with her hands. Piper guided her to the desk and helped her sit in the swivel chair before her knees gave way. "What should I do?"

Gavin pointed to the landline on the desk. "Nine-one-one."

"We already had one nasty arrest when the police picked up Dmitri and his friends. I don't want another incident with the local cops running around with guns blazing."

Distrust of authority? The attitude wasn't unusual among survivalists and preppers. Maybe he'd misjudged Chris's easygoing, back-to-nature stance. Tai was dangerous. A loose cannon. "If you'd rather, I'll contact the marshals in Beaverton for backup."

"That doesn't sound good, either. People around here value their privacy."

"It's the sensible thing to do," Piper said gently. "We need your help to locate Logan and Sofia. Can you tell us where they might go to hide. Maybe some place on the commune property? Or visiting friends who live nearby?"

With teary eyes, Chris looked up at Piper. "I don't know."

Though Gavin appreciated Piper's mellow approach to Chris, there were practical concerns to be addressed before he left them in the study and started his hunt for Tai. "When we were here before, I noticed that you have several vehicles. What's Logan driving?"

"After lunch, he took off in his Chevy truck. A 2007 Silverado, dark gray and kind of beat up. I can give you the license plate."

"That'd be helpful," he said. "Another question. I know you have a rifle. Any other guns?"

"Of course, I have guns. Twenty or more." Her tone implied that owning multiple guns was as normal as collecting stamps. "This is a farm where we raise chickens, goats, horses and a couple of milk cows. We need to be able to protect our livestock."

"Do you have a gun in this room?"

She yanked open the lower right desk drawer, lifted out a metal box and twirled the dial on a combination lock. "This is a Colt .45 revolver that belonged to my grandpa. I keep it close for sentimental reasons."

She lifted out a pewter-colored gun with a rose-wood grip.

"It's a beauty," Gavin said. "Is it loaded?"

"It will be." She took out a blue-velvet bag from the metal case, untied the fastening and dumped six silver bullets on the desktop. "A gun isn't much use if you don't have ammo."

Izzy rested her chin on Chris's leg as the older lady expertly loaded the revolver, slipping the silver bullets into the chambers and rotating the cylinder. He had no worries about Chris being able to defend herself. Piper, on the other hand, didn't have the training or the temperament to engage in a shoot-out. Her best protection was a lovable furball with the surprising ability to transform into *Cujo*.

"I didn't expect to run into Taimar when we came here," Gavin said, "but now that we've found him, I won't let him get away."

Piper lifted her chin. "How do we stop him?"

"When I leave," he said, "I want you to blockade the door so he can't get in. Duck behind the desk in case he starts firing wildly. In the unlikely event that he makes it into the room, go ahead and shoot him, Chris. Don't get fancy. Just aim for center mass and fire three times."

"You want me to kill him?"

"I want you and Piper to be safe."

"And Izzy," Chris said, smiling at the dog. "We don't want anything to happen to this pretty girl."

Before stepping into the hallway, Gavin took a long look at Piper, savoring the graceful tumble of her auburn hair and her heart-shaped face. His pulse jumped into high gear when he remembered the warmth of her body pressed against him. Though this wasn't the right time to think about how close they were becoming and how good it felt, he couldn't stop himself.

Using his SAT phone, he called DJ and advised him to dispatch a backup team to the Offenbach commune. "Beekman has the instructions on how to get here. And tell them not to come in with sirens blaring. There are civilians on the premises."

He ended the call and left the room. Through the windows, he saw that the red-and-gold sunset had faded into dusk with a few more overhead clouds but no rain. He wanted this chase to be over but forced himself to be patient and logical. Tai could very well be in this house. Gavin suspected the young man had been watching for him and Piper, and even Sofia, to appear. If so, he would have seen their arrival and would know where they were. Tai was impulsive; he might be foolish enough to come after them.

Chris's attractive cedar home had large rooms and high ceilings. When Gavin turned on lamps, the shadows stretched across the hardwood floors and created puddles of darkness behind sofas and under tables. Beretta in hand, he cleared each room on the first floor.

From inside the study, he heard Piper and Chris moving furniture and talking. They sounded upset, and he didn't want to get in the middle of whatever was bothering them. Their conversation was occasionally punctuated by snuffling noises from Izzy.

He returned to the front room with the two-story fieldstone fireplace, staircase and balcony. Searching on the second floor would be nearly impossible without making himself into an easy target. Instead, he took a position against the wall facing the front entryway where he settled into a profound silence and listened. Most of the floors were hardwood and prone to creaking. He heard someone or something moving across the upper level. There was the sound of a door closing. Would Tai hide until he was certain Gavin had left? Would he seek to use the element of surprise?

Gavin heard a scraping noise from the rear of the house behind the kitchen. Moving as stealthily as possible, he peeked around the corner from the front room toward the dining area where a long table stretched all the way to French doors onto a lighted terrace. Dark shadows obscured the corner behind the breakfront. He sensed movement from the kitchen.

The house reminded him of a maze with too many rooms and corridors that circled and twisted. He crept into the hallway outside the study. At the far end, a figure materialized from the darkness and then scooted away, heading toward the kitchen again. Staying close to the wall, Gavin slid down the hallway, passing the study. In the kitchen, he saw a shape, aimed his Beretta with both hands and...

"Chris? What are you doing here?"

"I got antsy." She turned on the overhead lights. "I hate sitting around and figured you could use some help."

She left Piper alone.

Gavin pivoted and swerved into the hallway just as Izzy burst into a frantic, ferocious howl. A tall, young man with wide shoulders in a plaid wool shirt stood outside the closed door to the study. The light from the front entry reflected off the rifle he held in his right hand.

"Freeze." Gavin braced his Beretta in both hands. "Federal marshal. Drop your weapon."

Tai whipped his head toward Gavin. His thick eyebrows lowered in a scowl and his mouth curved in a sneer that showed off his missing tooth. He said nothing.

"Drop the rifle," Gavin said. "Now."

"Nice to finally meet you in person, Marshal Mc-Queen." Tai rolled his eyes, an action that made him look very youthful, younger than Sofia. Why was he so nonchalant? Did he think they were playing a game? "Are you going to make me drop my gun?"

"Don't push me," Gavin said. "I will shoot."

Tai dropped his rifle on the floor. "It's not a real gun, anyway. Just a Taser."

With enough voltage to take down an elephant. Gavin shoved him up against the wall and patted him down, finding the Glock. "This appears to be a real weapon."

Izzy continued to bark. It sounded like she was

throwing herself against the door. From inside the study, Piper called out to them. "Is everything okay?"

Chris popped up at Gavin's elbow. "We've got everything under control. You can come out."

"No," Tai snapped. "Keep that devil dog away from me."

Behind the door, Gavin heard Piper talking to Izzy. The dog was calming down but not enough. Gavin pulled Tai's hands behind his back and fastened cuffs to his wrists. To Chris, he said, "I'm taking my prisoner onto the porch. Stay inside with Piper and Izzy. Can you follow that instruction?"

"Is that a snide comment?" She caressed the Colt .45 that she still held in her small hands. "I guess you didn't like the idea of me defending my home and property."

He wasn't about to argue with her. "Other cops, marshals and FBI will be here soon. I'll turn Tai over to them. Piper and Izzy and I will be on our way, unless you have some useful ideas about where your son might have taken Sofia."

Her eyes narrowed. "I really don't know."

Would she tell him if she did? Chris Offenbach was a difficult woman to figure out. He admired her independence, but she had a truly irritating stubborn streak. The fact that she had allowed Dmitri to stay at the commune worried him, and he hoped she wasn't involved in anything illegal.

On the porch, Gavin turned Tai to face him. Everybody, including this young man, had secrets. Gavin lacked the time to be subtle. "I was a little bit surprised by you, Tai. How come you gave up so easy?"

"Why should I struggle? You have the upper hand, and I'd rather not get beat up."

"But you don't mind fights," Gavin said. "You were a hockey player for the Ducks, a power forward."

A grin twitched at the edges of Tai's mouth. "In the rink, that's where I learned to choose my battles. There's no reason to get into it with you. You see, Mr. Marshal, I was in the house all along, and I overheard you tell Chris that Sofia had gone missing. Bad news for you. Worse news for me because my assignment was to find Sofia."

Gavin put the pieces together. "When you heard that she wasn't with us, you had no reason to put up a fuss."

Standing at the edge of the porch, Tai looked out at the landscaped area with the central bandstand. "She's a damn good singer, you know. I heard her a couple of times."

His opinion meant absolutely nothing to Gavin. Taimar Drako might think of himself as someone important, but he was nothing more than a low-level thug. "You're in deep trouble, Tai, about to be charged with attempted murder."

"Doesn't worry me. My grandpa has the world's greatest lawyers and they'll get me off with nothing more than a slap on the wrist."

When he thought of Marco's pain and suffering from gunshot wounds, Gavin hated to hear this snot-nosed kid make such a jaded comment. "Don't be so sure you'll get away with what you've done."

"Open your eyes, McQueen. My grandpa is a powerful man. After he's sprung from jail, he'll take care of me. Sofia and Marco caused some problems, but Ivanov will figure it out and get everything back on track. He's here in Oregon. Everything is going to work out for me."

Gavin studied Tai with outright disgust. "Here's something that puzzles me. Why didn't you take off and disappear as soon as you overheard us talking and knew Sofia wasn't around? Why did you hang around? Why were you lurking outside the door to the study?"

"Unfinished business." Tai stared at him with cold eyes that were very much like his grandfather. "I want to kill that damn dog."

Chapter Eighteen

When the dust settled at the Offenbach commune, Taimar had been arrested for attempted murder. Piper found herself at the gazebo bandstand in the central area with Gavin, DJ, Esposito and Izzy. There had been no reassuring phone calls from Sofia and no major changes—good or bad—in Marco's condition. The investigation had taken another turn, leaving her to worry about what came next for her and Gavin.

Joining the WITSEC program seemed excessive. True, she'd witnessed Taimar standing over Marco with a gun. But Marco had seen him, too. Her part in the crime didn't rise to the level of lifetime protection. Besides, WITSEC wasn't for her. She didn't want to uproot her entire life and start over in a new place when she'd settled into her current lifestyle in Oregon.

Where did her status as a nonwitness leave her with Gavin? If he wasn't professionally associated with her, would they continue to have a relationship? She hoped they could switch into a normal pattern that included dating, spending a day together or taking in a movie. She could make him a gourmet beef stroganoff with truffles.

A lovely dream, but they were still far away from having a peaceful, uncomplicated relationship. Danger still surrounded them. Ivanov was at large and planning a hostage exchange And Sofia had disappeared. Thinking of the sixteen-year-old alone and unprotected caused Piper's stomach to clench. They needed to find her. Soon.

She and Izzy stood at the railing in the bandshell and watched the three marshals pace around a dozen still-blooming rosebushes. Gavin didn't have DJ's husky build or Esposito's taste in clothing, but Marshal McQueen drew her attention like a handsome male magnet. His loose-limbed gait and easy posture excited her. He was the only one of the three who literally stopped and smelled the roses.

When he waved her over to join them, Izzy went first, tail wagging every step of the way.

Gavin lightly touched Piper's arm, sending an electric buzz across the surface of her skin. "You should hear this, Piper."

"About the Dragons," Esposito said. "They like big, grandiose operations that make headlines. The *troika* intended to shut down Liberty International Airport in Newark. Ivanov staged a jailbreak from a formerly impregnable penitentiary. They go for the big gestures."

"Ivanov has selected five possible airfields,"

Gavin said, "but he won't announce the location until the day of the scheduled exchange."

"Tomorrow?" Piper guessed.

"Tomorrow or the next day. When he tells us where he will be landing, he'll also give a time. The hostage exchange won't commence until we've deposited five million bucks in a numbered offshore account."

"Appallingly specific," she said.

"There's more," Gavin said. "Yuri Drako will be completely exonerated with all charges dismissed."

"What about Ivanov the pilot?"

"He was convicted of second-degree murder and he escaped from the penitentiary. He won't get a pardon, but he'll be allowed safe passage out of the country."

"Unbelievable." Shaking her head, Piper looked from DJ to Esposito to Gavin. Their circumstances seemed grim. "You left one thing out, something important. They don't have hostages."

Esposito scoffed. "That's a nasty hole in their plot."

Funny how things had worked out. Dear little Sofia had managed to disrupt these guys more than any of the law enforcement officers involved. By disappearing, she'd thrown a wrench into the well-oiled scheme. Piper looked up at Gavin. "Where do we go from here?"

"We find Sofia," he said. "And I know where we should start."

Moments later, she, Izzy and Gavin boarded the SUV. He set a course toward the Yamhill forests and her cabin. More than once, Sofia had told them she felt at peace in Piper's home. It was a place to start.

Izzy rested her front paws on the center console and watched their progress through the windshield as the SUV jostled along on the twisting, narrow roads from the commune to the main road.

Piper wondered if they'd ever learn the identity of the rat who had been feeding information to Yuri Drako in prison. The first time she'd met Esposito, she'd felt certain that he was the double agent. Anybody as slick and smooth as the marshal from Jersey would have no problem juggling several identities.

"I made the right decision," Gavin said. "Putting DJ in charge was a good move. He's taken on the responsibility like a champ."

"His new wife might not be happy about having him spend more time away from home."

"Chelsey is understanding. They'll work out the details."

The early days in a relationship seemed like the first steps in a grand adventure. In the early days of her marriage to the scumbag, she'd had a marvelous time turning their small apartment into a home and discovering all the nuances of living with another person. Accidentally, she'd fed him peanut butter cookies and activated his allergy. If she'd known how badly the cookies would affect him, she could have force fed him another nine or ten to trigger an anaphylactic shock. Would have saved her all the trouble of getting a divorce. "Do you have allergies?" she asked.

"Hay fever in the spring. You?"

"Not a thing."

Never would she purposely hurt Gavin, and she suspected the same was true from his perspective. They rode a distance in comfortable silence while her thoughts sorted themselves out. A couple of times, she noticed headlights following them through the night. "I hope we find her at the cabin. If she gets Logan to take her there, she knows where the key is hidden."

"Wait a minute." He halted at a stop sign, turned toward her and studied her expression. "You've been wanting to go back to your cabin from the first moment I saw you."

She remembered that first moment when her brain registered the obvious fact that Gavin was a tall, well-built, manly man. And possibly an adversary. "I remember."

"This trip to the cabin," he said. "Do you really think Sofia is there. Or is this a con?"

"I won't lie to you. I'd be thrilled to pick up a change of clothes, shoes and underwear. But I'm not trying to trick you. I would never use this terrible situation with Sofia as an excuse."

"And if she's not there, we'll have to think of somewhere else."

"The options are limited. Staying with friends is always a possibility. Or getting a room in a motel." She didn't like that alternative. Sofia and Logan were so young. "I suppose they could camp or sleep in the back of his truck."

"Staying at your cabin sounds like the best choice."

She reached over and scratched between Izzy's ears. "We're going home. Not forever, not even for very long, but I promise I'll grab a couple of bags of your favorite treat."

The dog licked her face and then turned to Gavin.

He held up a hand. "No licking. I love you, Izzy, but I'm not a fan of dog slobber."

Her directions into the Yamhill National Forest led them down a winding path that bordered a rippling creek amid moss-covered pines, spreading ferns, autumnal-colored shrubs and fiery-red maples. The closer they got, the more she felt the warmth of homecoming. Izzy picked up on her mood and wiggled around in the back seat.

She watched the play of emotion on Gavin's face. If he hated this place, she'd be heartbroken. But she didn't need to worry. His quiet smile stretched from ear to ear. And his dark eyes caught the reflected glow from the cloudless night.

"You like it here," she said.

"Much as I hate to admit that Sofia is right, she nailed it. Your forest feels safe."

"I hope she's here." Though Sofia's disappearance wakened a burden of dread, she couldn't help feeling hopeful anticipation. "She's got to be here."

"If not," Gavin said, "we'll go in a different direction. Maybe Frick and Frack have come up with a viable lead. We might need to talk with Marco."

That was a conversation she'd rather avoid. Papa Marco would go berserk when he found out that his daughter was on the run. "There are so many places she and Logan could go."

"Oregon has a lot of hideouts."

"Have you always lived here?"

"Among other places," he said. "My favorite place is the shore, especially during the annual King Tides when the surf rises ten feet or more and crashes against the harbors and beaches. And I love the coastal forests on the western side of the Cascades."

His deep voice soothed her like a lullaby. "Take a right up here, then one final right."

No lights were on in her small log cabin that nestled cozily amid towering ponderosa pine. Moonlight sparkled against the window glass. If Sofia and Logan had come here, they were long gone.

She unsnapped her seat belt and climbed out. After flinging open the back door so Izzy could dash through the familiar forest, Piper exhaled a frustrated sigh and leaned against the SUV. When Gavin joined her, she wrapped her arms around his neck and melted against him. "I really thought she'd be here."

"Struck out again."

He held her tightly but with gentle consideration. When they kissed, they shared the same breath. Their hearts beat as one.

He nuzzled her earlobe and murmured, "We'll find them."

"We have to."

"In the meantime…"

He rained kisses upon her. Though there was a

huge temptation to spend the night here. In her bed-room. Under the fluffy comforter. Making love.

But they needed to concentrate on finding Sofia. Inside the house, Gavin pulled out his phone and started checking with Beekman and DJ and Frick and Frack.

Though it wasn't awfully cold, he insisted on building a fire and went to the shed to pick up a couple of logs while she prepared her special blend of decaf coffee with cocoa and whipped cream. From outside, she heard Izzy barking.

"Calm down, silly mutt."

Though she had no nearby neighbors who might be disturbed, Piper didn't want Izzy waking the whole forest. She rummaged through the freezer, looking for something to go with the coffee and found a loaf of homemade zucchini bread, which she popped into the microwave to thaw.

Standing at the kitchen counter, she looked toward the front door. What was taking Gavin so long? The door swung open.

"About time," she teased.

The man framed in her doorway was a stranger. He swept a bow. "Allow me to introduce myself. I am Tom Ivanov."

"Where's Gavin?"

"Don't worry about your lover." Ivanov spoke clear English without an accent. "He is doing bet-ter than you, my dear. You will take Sofia's place as my hostage."

He stalked toward her and she grabbed a bread

knife from the counter. With one sweep of his powerful arm, he knocked the weapon from her hand.

Standing behind him was another man. She recognized Phillip Esposito. The marshal from Jersey.
He must be working with Ivanov, must be the rat.

But Esposito was holding a gun, threatening Ivanov, trying to arrest him. Not a rat, after all.

A stun gun pressed against the side of her neck.
She went unconscious.

Chapter Nineteen

Gavin awoke to the pain. His arms and shoulder joints ached from his wrists being cuffed behind his back. The inside of his head throbbed with each tortured breath. And Izzy licked his face.

DJ hovered over him. "You're going to be okay."

"Piper. Where's Piper?"

"Gone."

The anguish of losing her was worse than any physical wound he could have suffered. His eyelids shuttered and he wished for sleep, endless sleep. They'd been so close to making love. She'd shown him her bed. Her blue eyes had twinkled with the sexiest invite of all time.

"She's the hostage," DJ said. "Ivanov has her."

Not dead. There was reason for hope. He forced himself to sit up. "I want these cuffs off. We've got to find her. Can't let that bastard win."

A young man wearing a black EMS jacket with reflective tape squatted beside Gavin and unlocked the handcuffs. With gloved fingers, he gently probed a wound above his eyebrow and asked the obvious question. "Does this hurt?"

"I'm fine." He pushed the medic away. With a mighty effort, he got himself upright for about ten seconds before his knees buckled and he collapsed onto a rough bench beside an outdoor shed. Gavin touched the painful spot on his head. His fingers came away bloody. "What the hell happened?"

"You were attacked," DJ said. "Before you went unconscious, you hit an emergency alert button on your SAT phone that gave us your location. When we tried calling you back, Ivanov answered. He said he was taking Piper to use for the hostage exchange. There'll be three of them. Piper and two pilots who own the plane Ivanov stole."

A beautiful blond woman wearing a standard FBI jacket and a stethoscope around her neck sat on the bench beside him. Gavin thought he recognized her. He squinted at her and then recalled. "Alexandra. The nurse, you're Drako's nurse at the Sheridan penitentiary."

"Special Agent Lily Godwin," she said as an introduction. "I didn't think I was that memorable."

Though she wore a shapeless T-shirt and khakis, the blonde wasn't someone who could easily be forgotten. She listened to his chest through a stethoscope.

"You're a double agent," Gavin said. "Feeding info to Drako and gathering intel for us."

"Stating the obvious, McQueen." She lowered the stethoscope and leaned close to examine the wound on his forehead. "I'm a certified RN, and I advise you to get some stitches in that contusion unless you like facial scars."

"Just slap a bandage on it so I won't get an infection."

"You're the boss." She dug into a medical bag, put on a pair of purple latex gloves and opened a sanitized wipe to clean his wound. "The Dracula marks from the two-prong stun gun will go away by themselves."

"Do I have a concussion?"

"Most likely."

"I wouldn't mind taking a painkiller that didn't make me woozy."

"When something like that is invented, I'll let you know. For now, you'll have to settle for extra-strength ibuprofen." She dabbed at his wound, and he winced. "I'd also advise you to go on bed rest under a doctor's care for a few days. But I doubt you'll back down from the chase."

"He has Piper," Gavin said. "I won't abandon her."

"Moof," Izzy said.

DJ petted the dog between her floppy ears. "I was shocked that Izzy survived an encounter with a cold-blooded murderer like Ivanov. Apparently, the Russian has a soft spot in his heart for truffle hounds. He shut her in the shed while he dealt with Piper."

Gavin knew Izzy—a trained attack dog—would switch to her *Cujo* identity if anyone tried to harm her owner. "The mutt didn't try to protect me."

"You're still alive," DJ pointed out. "Esposito wasn't so lucky."

He explained as much as he knew about the death of the marshal from Jersey. Using intel from his confidential informant, Esposito had arranged a meeting with Ivanov, hoping he could get the whole hostage exchange turned around. He'd had long discussions with the US Marshals Service legal advisers about what sort of deal he could offer the escaped convict.

"He should have talked to you," Gavin said.

"Esposito was one of those guys who like to go it alone. No partners. No backup."

And he'd paid the price. Ivanov had shot him in the forehead, execution-style.

Lily finished with the bandage and sat back to admire her handiwork. "A scar on the forehead might be kind of sexy."

"I thought Esposito was the rat," Gavin said, "but it was you."

"Not a rat. I'm a well-trained undercover agent who also happens to be a medical professional." She handed Gavin a container of painkillers and a bottle of water. "I have two more important details about the hostage exchange. Are you ready, guys?"

DJ switched his phone to Record and held it up for her to speak into. "Ready."

"You're cute," she said.

"And very married," he said.

Gavin exhaled a groan. "Can we move along?"

"Number one," she said, "Ivanov will expect a

code word to identify Yuri Drako. It's *'ura.'* A Russian battle cry."

DJ tried the word a couple of times. "Easy enough. What else?"

"This is harder," she said. "Ivanov wants to ask several questions about their shared history. Yuri needs to respond in Russian."

"Why?"

"Ivanov knows Yuri is ill and looks different from the last time they were together. He doesn't want you guys to sneak in a ringer."

Gavin recognized the problem. Slowly, he forced himself to push off from the bench and stand. He stared straight ahead, waiting for the world to stop spinning. They'd figure out a way to rescue the hostages. There was no other choice. Until Piper was safe in his arms, he would not rest.

LAST NIGHT, Piper remembered, the sunset had been a brilliant crimson. Red sky at night meant she should have been basking in good luck, but that wasn't the way things had turned out. How could everything have gone so wrong? Last night, she'd been minutes away from making love to Gavin and sealing the nascent attraction that had been building between them. And now? Now, she sat in a padded lounge chair in a small Beechcraft corporate jet. Silver duct tape bound her wrists and ankles, but she felt okay except for the two wounds from the stun gun and residual stiffness from the resulting seizure. Every muscle and nerve had tensed in a full-body charley horse.

Sitting across from her in two similar chairs were the owners of this Beechcraft—a couple of men in their early forties who dressed in the outdoorsy style of Abercrombie & Fitch. Both showed a decent level of fitness, and she hoped they'd figure out a way to overpower Ivanov and get them off this jet. In spite of the duct tape over their mouths, they needed to find a way to communicate and make an escape plan. She wasn't ready to give up.

Peering through the porthole window, she tried to figure out what time it was. Would the exchange take place today or tomorrow? She preferred to get it over with. Twenty-four hours wouldn't change her situation too much.

When Ivanov wandered back into the cabin, she raised her hands above her head and waved him over. He draped his long arm across the top edge of her chair and leaned down. "What's the problem?"

She mimed pulling the tape off her mouth.

"You wish to speak?"

Ivanov reached down, grasped an edge of duct tape and ripped. She gasped in pain but also relief. Breathing the air felt delicious. "Thank you," she said. "May I please have water?"

"Of course." His boisterous voice echoed in the small cabin. "I want my sweet hostages to be comfy. *Da*?"

As soon as her two companions saw what she'd accomplished, they started making similar noises and demands. Ivanov swiveled his head and glared at them.

"I have an idea," she said. "Why don't you remove the tape from my wrists and ankles? Then I can serve you gentlemen. I believe I saw vodka in the cabinet beside the kitchenette."

"Vodka?" Ivanov was interested. "You will be a waitress?"

"I would be honored."

Piper had spent several years working with smug, insensitive, corporate males who looked upon every woman as a server. She could use that prejudice.

Ivanov was easily convinced. He cut her duct tape, pulled her to her feet and lowered himself into her comfortable lounge chair. "Bring me vodka with a twist, and something to eat."

She did exactly as he asked. After another drink, he agreed that the other men should be freed from their bonds to join with him in drinking. There wasn't much to eat. Mostly crackers and canned anchovies, tuna and caviar, which was fine for Ivanov.

She coddled him, cossetted him and complimented him on his clever plan to free Yuri Drako with a hostage exchange. With careful nudging, her comments led the Russian to admit that the exchange would take place today. In less than two hours.

THE TIME HAD been set. The airfield selected. And Gavin had figured out a dangerous scam to outwit Ivanov. Instead of bringing Yuri Drako from the prison in Sheridan for the exchange, Marco would pose as the old Dragon to answer Ivanov's questions in native Russian. He would be pushed to the

door of the jet in a wheelchair by none other than
his regular nurse, Special Agent Lily Godwin, who
would be armed.

The unexpected happy consequence of working
with Marco was the return of Sofia who had been
hiding in the hospital with Logan. They'd tried other
places where she could disappear, but her concern for
her papa led her back to Overton Hospital.

When the final preparations were in place, Sofia
apologized to Gavin. She was frightened for her dad
but proud of him at the same time. She crouched
down beside his wheelchair. "Daddy, are you strong
enough to pull this off?"

"I've always been capable of doing the right thing."
He squeezed her hand. "It's our fault that Piper is in
such extreme danger. We can't turn our backs and
walk away."

"I know," she said.

"If you learn nothing more from this experience,
I want you to realize how important it is to think of
other people and consider their opinions."

Silently, she nodded. For once, Sofia listened.

AT THE APPOINTED hour of four o'clock, the Beechcraft swooped down onto the tarmac on the small
airfield and taxied to a stop. All the runways had
been cleared, and hangars were locked tightly. There
was an array of law enforcement vehicles and am-
bulances.

As per Ivanov's instructions, the five million had
already been wired and received in the offshore ac-

count. Everyone had stayed in their vehicles, except Marco, in the wheelchair posing as Yuri Drako, his beautiful blond nurse and Marshal Gavin McQueen. His heart was in his throat. These moments would decide who lived and who died.

A staircase descended from the plane. Ivanov swaggered out and almost tripped as he descended. Waving both arms, he called out to the man in the wheelchair. "Give me the battle cry."

"Ura," Marco shouted. He coughed before repeating, *"Ura, comrade."*

Ivanov started toward them. "You don't look good, Drako."

Marco swore at him in fluent Russian. "I've been ill."

Gavin held up his hand. "You come no farther until I see the hostages."

"Of course."

Ivanov clapped his hands, and Gavin saw the most wonderful sight he'd ever experienced. Two men who looked like an advertisement for L.L. Bean emerged from the Beechcraft. Then Piper walked carefully down the staircase to the tarmac. Though he was too far away to see the blue of her eyes, he knew the cerulean color.

Ivanov asked his questions in Russian, and Marco easily responded in the native tongue he'd learned from his mother. Gradually, they moved closer and closer.

Playing her part as Alexandra the sexy nurse, Special Agent Lily Godwin flashed a bit of cleavage in a highly effective distraction.

When Ivanov was only ten yards away, Gavin revealed his gun. And so did Lily. Marco got out of the wheelchair and let loose with a stream of Russian curses.

Ivanov wouldn't give up without a fight. He pulled out his Kalashnikov and turned to point the assault rifle at Piper. Gavin fired first. Without hesitation.

Before Ivanov hit the tarmac, Piper dashed past Marco and his double-agent nurse. She leaped into Gavin's waiting arms.

"Never let me go," she whispered.

"Not in a million years," he said.

Izzy said, "Moof."

A MONTH LATER, Piper woke on Thanksgiving morning with a heart full of love and gratitude. The threat from Yuri and the Dragons had been squashed, Taimar Drako was still in jail awaiting his trial for attempted murder, the Barbieri family—they decided to stick with that name—was no longer under threat and US Marshal Gavin McQueen had moved into her secluded cabin in the forest. She rolled over on the bed and gazed into his wide-open eyes.

"You're awake," she murmured.

"I always sleep with one eye open." He caressed the line of her jaw and ran his thumb across her lower lip. "In law enforcement, it's an occupational requirement to be forever alert."

"You're so noble," she teased. "Will you maintain

that level of high alert when you've left the US Marshals Service to be a trooper?"

"Absolutely." His arms encircled her, and the warmth of his embrace surrounded her. "Keeping you safe is a full-time job."

The decision to change jobs hadn't been a difficult one. Gavin didn't want his work to revolve around establishing false identities and keeping secrets. As a sergeant in the Oregon state police, he could be straight-forward, direct and totally honest.

Piper approved. She especially liked that he'd be working from Yamhill and the central headquarters were in Salem which wasn't far away. Moving in with her had made perfect sense.

Apparently, Izzy agreed. With a cheerful bark, the dog bounded into the bedroom and circled the bed, wagging her tail and pushing one paw onto the comforter. She'd been well-trained to *not* jump on the bed.

She kissed Gavin on the forehead and climbed from the bed. "I need to finish cooking. I'd like to get to Marco's house early to help with the turkey. We're making roasted walnut and truffle dressing."

"More truffles."

"You like them. Don't pretend you don't." She'd already made a truffle pudding, truffle salad and truffle tapenade with extra virgin olive oil.

"This is going to be a crowd."

"DJ and his wife, Chelsey, Logan and his mom, chef Rosa, Sofia's friends from school and Marco's doctor."

"Nobody refuses a feast at the home of a renowned chef."

When Marco opted out of WITSEC, his life had expanded, and his talent was on full display. The same went for Sofia who had signed up with a talent agent in the hopes of launching a career.

The potential for danger had diminished when Yuri's health took a turn for the worse and his son who lived in Devil's Lake was totally occupied with clearing his reputation and providing his son with legal representation. Ivanov recovered from his wounds and was incarcerated in a Super Max facility.

Piper went to the window and opened the curtain. Outside, the sun shone brilliantly. A perfect Thanksgiving.

When Gavin came up behind her, she snuggled against his bare, muscular chest. Life didn't get much better than this.

* * * * *

Get 3 FREE REWARDS!

We'll send you 2 FREE Books plus a FREE Mystery Gift.

FREE
Value Over
$20

Both the **Harlequin Intrigue®** and **Harlequin® Romantic Suspense** series feature compelling novels filled with heart-racing action-packed romance that will keep you on the edge of your seat.

YES! Please send me 2 FREE novels from the Harlequin Intrigue or Harlequin Romantic Suspense series and my FREE gift (gift is worth about $10 retail). After receiving them, if I don't wish to receive any more books, I can return the shipping statement marked "cancel." If I don't cancel, I will receive 6 brand-new Harlequin Intrigue Larger-Print books every month and be billed just $6.49 each in the U.S. or $6.99 each in Canada, a savings of at least 13% off the cover price, or 4 brand-new Harlequin Romantic Suspense books every month and be billed just $5.49 each in the U.S. or $6.24 each in Canada, a savings of at least 12% off the cover price. It's quite a bargain! Shipping and handling is just 50¢ per book in the U.S. and $1.25 per book in Canada.* I understand that accepting the 2 free books and gift places me under no obligation to buy anything. I can always return a shipment and cancel at any time by calling the number below. The free books and gift are mine to keep no matter what I decide.

Choose one:

☐ **Harlequin Intrigue Larger-Print**
(199/399 BPA GRMX)

☐ **Harlequin Romantic Suspense**
(240/340 BPA GRMX)

☐ **Or Try Both!**
(199/399 & 240/340 BPA GRQD)

Name (please print)

Address   Apt. #

City   State/Province   Zip/Postal Code

Email: Please check this box ☐ if you would like to receive newsletters and promotional emails from Harlequin Enterprises ULC and its affiliates. You can unsubscribe anytime.

Mail to the **Harlequin Reader Service:**
IN U.S.A.: P.O. Box 1341, Buffalo, NY 14240-8531
IN CANADA: P.O. Box 603, Fort Erie, Ontario L2A 5X3

Want to try 2 free books from another series? Call 1-800-873-8635 or visit www.ReaderService.com.

*Terms and prices subject to change without notice. Prices do not include sales taxes, which will be charged (if applicable) based on your state or country of residence. Canadian residents will be charged applicable taxes. Offer not valid in Quebec. This offer is limited to one order per household. Books received may not be as shown. Not valid for current subscribers to the Harlequin Intrigue or Harlequin Romantic Suspense series. All orders subject to approval. Credit or debit balances in a customer's account(s) may be offset by any other outstanding balance owed by or to the customer. Please allow 4 to 6 weeks for delivery. Offer available while quantities last.

Your Privacy—Your information is being collected by Harlequin Enterprises ULC, operating as Harlequin Reader Service. For a complete summary of the information we collect, how we use this information and to whom it is disclosed, please visit our privacy notice located at corporate.harlequin.com/privacy-notice. From time to time we may also exchange your personal information with reputable third parties. If you wish to opt out of this sharing of your personal information, please visit readerservice.com/consumerschoice or call 1-800-873-8635. Notice to California Residents—Under California law, you have specific rights to control and access your data. For more information on these rights and how to exercise them, visit corporate.harlequin.com/california-privacy.

HIHRS23

HARLEQUIN
PLUS

Try the best multimedia subscription service for romance readers like you!

Read, Watch and Play.

Experience the easiest way to get the romance content you crave.

Start your **FREE TRIAL** at
<u>www.harlequinplus.com/freetrial</u>.